CONTEN

Sowerby's London,
Sale of Unique (And Often) Mysterious Objects

Lot No. 586

A Notebook: found in highly dangerous circumstances but we cannot reveal the source for fear of reprisals against its owner. We believe, though it is impossible to prove, that this Notebook has returned from the Other World.

N.B. No responsibility can be taken by Sowerby's for the security of any future owner. The Chief Executive of Sowerby's is taking an extended leave of absence, and will not be contactable on this or any other subject, for a very long time. In plain English, if you are interested in this Notebook, *you are on your own...*

<u>To: The Finder of This Notebook</u>

If you are *already* dead, you will find little of interest in this Notebook. For at least some of my story you will have experienced first-hand. If, however, you are still living then prepare yourself for what you will find within these pages.

For this is an experience beyond the power of imagination...

Simon de Bruin

This book is dedicated to my mum, Violet
And my sisters, Hazel & Helen

Chapter 1

The Black Iron Gates

The double wrought-iron gates loomed tall and menacing; old ivy had trailed and trained itself around the age-eaten and crumbling bars, which were barely visible in the greyish, vaporous night mist. A deep and penetrating stillness pervaded the air, as if no living thing existed in this place.

From far below, I stared up at the unfamiliar scene. *Where was I?* Glancing round, I noticed a long, high wall attached to the gates, stretching out on either side of them. The enveloping mist didn't allow me to see how far the walls ran or indeed what lay behind them. I shivered, and pulled my jacket closer to my shaking body. It was only then I noticed the rips in it and a hole in the knee of my trousers. *What had happened?* I was normally *very* tidy and never fell over. My mother had taught me to look after my clothes, as there was little money to buy more after my father died.

Returning my gaze to the gate, I now noticed a long, rusting chain, hanging at the side and partially covered by the ivy; attached to it was a handle – a very old, ornate handle which seemed to invite me to pull it.

As I couldn't see a single, breathing person, I tentatively took hold of it (by standing on my toes), held my breath and then pulled on the chain. It made a disappointingly low clanging noise, which echoed far beyond the gates.

I waited. Nothing happened.

I was trying to make up my mind if it would be rude to ring again, when I heard a noise. Very faint at first, but drawing closer; a type of scuffling and what sounded like someone forcing their way through tangled undergrowth. Soon, I saw a faint glow, which steadily grew brighter until, finally, the bent figure of an old man appeared out of the mist behind the gates. Although his face was cast in shadow, I could see he didn't look pleased. I also noticed he was somehow insubstantial, as if he might float away at any moment.

Holding a cane lamp higher to get a better look, he exclaimed in a loud, irritable voice: 'What time o' night do ye think this is, boy? Couldn't thee hav waited 'til morn?'

'I...I couldn't...I mean I didn't...'

'Couldn't, didn't, make up yer mind, can't ye? Furst Timers, they're alwus the same...no consideration fer ma rest...no idee...'

I took a step backwards.

The man squared his shoulders.

'Name?' he snapped.

'Simon...Simon de Bruin.'

The man grunted, consulted a lengthy, egg-yolk coloured scroll he was clutching, finally found what he wanted, and grunted again.

'D.O.D.?' he barked, his voice ricocheting across the still night. A grey quill had materialized from somewhere, perhaps from underneath his moth-eaten black gown.

I looked around but I was still alone. 'Are you talking to *me?*' I asked, my voice quivering.

'Who else?' came the angry reply. 'See anyone else daft enough to be out at this time o' night, not with so many hell-hounds abroad anyways…'

'Hell-hounds?' I asked nervously. 'What are they? Are they… are they…dangerous?'

'They may well be, if ye don't stop yer bladderin' and answer ma question. Noo, fer the second time, D.O.D.?' he bellowed.

My knees began to knock together. I was certain of this because I could hear them. A distant sound quivered in the night air; was it a horn of some kind?

'Fer the third time, Date Of Death? I need yer answer *now*, boy 'cause the hell-hounds are comin' fer sure; that's their soundin' horn.'

Suddenly, I felt a burning pain in my lower right leg, and heard loud snarling and yelping; I screamed with pain and kicked out frantically – but I could see nothing. My attackers were invisible and then I was falling, falling…

Chapter 2

A Ghostly College

Grey light streamed in through three large windows – the brightness attacked my eyes as I attempted to open them. I felt I could sleep forever.

Through my eye-slits, I discovered I was in bed in a long, narrow room, with bare walls and faded curtains on the windows; there were two other single beds. All were neatly made up with white sheets and pale blue covers. I was the only occupant. I began to shiver. Where was I? How did I get here? Images of my mother frantic with worry flashed across my brain. Would I ever see her again?

A small, plump woman bustled into the room, wearing an ankle-length black dress. It was partially covered by a white apron trimmed with frill. A black lace cap sat neatly on her head. She carried a basin, full to the brim with steaming hot water. She frowned slightly as she hurried in my direction, but stopped when she saw my eyes were open and said:

'There you are, my dear, awake at last! I thought, for sure, you'd sleep all day. We've looked after your leg wound, it isn't too serious considering, but I expect you're exhausted. The journey can really take it out of you. Why, I remember my own passing as if it was only yesterday, and that was well over a hundred years ago...'

Her voice trailed off. I must have looked as horrified as I felt.

'Now, don't you worry your head about anything, dear,' she rushed on. 'It'll all work out, you'll see. It's not so bad here, once you get used to it...'

'*But where am I?*' I asked, now fully awake. 'That man at the gate, he asked a question, he asked me...' I stopped, unable to find the words.

The woman gently placed the basin on the locker beside my bed, her skirts making a not unpleasant rustling noise as she moved. She sat down beside me and put her arms around my shaking shoulders. 'You're so thin,' she said. I was often told that but somehow I didn't mind hearing it from her, and unconsciously found myself leaning into her welcoming embrace. But something was wrong. I couldn't actually *feel* her arms around me. Instead of normal body heat, there was only a slight chill. I pulled back and sat up straight, instinctively moving backwards against the pillows for support. I folded my arms across my chest and only then noticed I was wearing a blue, striped nightshirt. Just like the picture in one of my favourite books, *A Christmas Carol*. Slightly hesitant, I raised my hand to my head. Somehow, I wasn't surprised to discover I was also wearing a nightcap.

What is this crazy world? I couldn't help thinking. *I want to go home – now.* But the woman had other ideas.

'I'm Mrs. Honeydew, the matron,' she said gently. 'I help the new ones, like you, settle in. Help them get over the shock of their passing. I hope you're not too upset, dear.'

But of course, I was upset, who wouldn't be? For the *second* time I'd been told I was dead. I pulled the scratchy sheets close to my chin, and held onto them for dear life. At least they felt real enough but I wasn't so sure about the woman. She didn't look quite *normal,* as if she was only a faded version of her original self; as if she wasn't *quite all there.* Although, I was now beginning to think that perhaps I wasn't quite all there either. I could be imagining this, or it was a dream. Yes, that was it, I was at home asleep in our cottage, and Mother would soon be shaking me awake for school. I closed my eyes. Soon things would be back to normal. I almost looked forward to hearing her complain I'd be late again. And I definitely wanted to hear Sparky, my wire-haired terrier, barking.

I didn't particularly like school but Farranfoe wasn't a bad village. It had everything you'd want, even its own busy harbour. Plenty of ships called as it was one of the few ports on the west coast of Ireland. All in all, it was an okay place to live, but now it seemed absolutely fantastic.

But as it turned out, it wasn't that simple.

'Of course,' continued Mrs. Honeydew, 'we've been waiting for *you* for centuries, Simon. The de Bruins have been associated with the college for many years…'

I opened my eyes and caught sight of the bed on the opposite side of the room. Oh, no, I was still here. 'How did you know my name?' I asked weakly, ashamed the shaking hadn't stopped.

Mrs. Honeydew laughed, and when she did her face lit up. I couldn't help thinking that she must have been pretty when she was young and quickly followed this thought with: yes and when she was alive! But I was missing what she was saying.

'...*everyone* knows the de Bruin name around here. Don't you know the history between your family and this college?' she asked, a note of incredulity creeping into her voice.

'No. Nobody ever mentioned it,' I said, my voice breaking. 'What do you mean, I'm in a college? Perhaps,' I said, as firmly as I could manage, throwing back the sheet and revealing a heavily bandaged leg, 'it's time I went home. Mother will be worr...'

Angry shouts came from outside the windows, as if from a large unruly crowd. I stopped and glanced nervously at the matron, who hurried over to the nearest window. She pressed her nose against the pane, and in doing so had a clear view of the central square, around which clustered many of the college's buildings.

'They're coming,' she said in a calm voice. 'There's no need to be frightened.'

But I wasn't frightened, I was terrified. *What was this crazy world I'd stumbled into?*

Chapter 3

Gauntley

All morning, the college had been alive with rumours (or as alive as a college can be when it's full of dead people). The news that the new arrival was none other than Simon de Bruin had sent the inhabitants, some of them ghostly residents for centuries, into a tailspin. By midday, fact and fiction had intertwined to the extent that the new boy was reputed to have single-handedly slain a thousand witches in the Nubian Wars, was both a breeder and trainer of dragons, and spoke fifteen languages (which included Swahili and a Moorish dialect now spoken by only three hundred people).

The Provost, Professor Rufus Gantley or, Gauntley as he was more generally known, hobbled around his apartments overlooking the old moated entrance to the college. He was both excited and worried. He'd heard the rumours circulating about the youngest de Bruin for years, but being a prudent man, he didn't know what to believe. 'Cogswattle and piffle,' he muttered to himself. 'Best get this over with, I suppose.' Waiting in the hallway outside his office were the eight most Senior Council members of the college, each one deeply suspicious of the new arrival but also overcome with curiosity to see him. Dr. Josiaph Funkelweede, D.O.L.T, N.I.T.-W.I.T. (3rd Level) was particularly curious; he was convinced that a de Bruin would be of immense help with his academic research. Dr. Funkelweede had spent his entire life (and death) writing a paper on dodos, which he was considering calling, *Dodos: Our Future,* or *Our Future is Dodo.* At the present time, he was leaning towards the latter.

The Provost glanced at his appearance in an oval, spotted mirror in a dark corner of the room. He tried to run a shaky hand through his long, white hair, but without success. There were far too many knots in it, and he couldn't even remember the last time he'd attempted to comb it. He sighed, as he surveyed his stick-thin, slightly bent frame and generally dilapidated appearance; he'd be the first to admit four hundred years as a ghost had done him no favours. He dreaded to think what he'd look like after another four hundred. Still, his appearance was the least of his worries.

The deputation of Provost and College Council glided slowly across Front Square, a grassy area surrounded by cobblestoned pathways. As the procession made its way, the Provost's stick tapped a rhythm and the rest of the college (uninvited) fell in behind the main party: former students, lecturers, librarians, and catering staff. Essentially, everyone who had either attended the college as a student or worked there since its foundation followed in his wake; all had returned to the college the moment they died. All had been shocked by this turn of events.

****

As if the last few hours weren't terrifying enough, I was startled to see heads and shoulders, followed by bodies floating in through the walls of my room. Very quickly, a crowd of ghosts amassed around my bed, rank on rank, some standing, some sitting, several lying on the empty beds; two even sat on the brass headboard behind my head, swinging their feet and occasionally hitting me a wallop. I couldn't believe the strange scene before me. I'd never seen anything like it. They all wore clothes from another era; they were all *from* another era. Fashions across the centuries blurred before my eyes; women in crinolines and men in top hats and frock coats. Many wore black gowns and mortar boards. There was a fair smattering of ruffs, monks' habits and suits of armour. However, while their dress was certainly out of the ordinary, more noticeably, some of the ghosts were missing noses and several had only one ear. It gave them a strange lopsided appearance.

The large, silent, ghostly crowd floated several inches above the floor. Some looked friendly, some hostile; all were curious.

I was terrified.

Professor Gantley held out a vein-encrusted hand, and introduced himself. 'Thou mayest call me Rufus,' he whispered, in a paper-thin voice. I couldn't help noticing he had only one ear.

'This is Simon de Bruin,' he explained to the assembled crowd. They murmured a ghostly welcome and a few smiled. 'Ye all know what this means for the college,' continued the Provost. 'We now have a fighting chance of beating Halbizia.' There was a round of applause from the crowd, who noticeably rallied at the old man's words.

But who is Halbizia? asked my numbed brain. And what had this to do with me? It was difficult to concentrate on what the old fuddy-duddy was saying, as a girl, about my own age, floated at the front. She'd caught my attention as she looked more like a boy than a girl. Her long blonde hair was tied up in two pigtails and in her ears were large round earrings that jangled when she turned her head, but she wore boy's clothes: baggy trousers, a loose shirt and leather waistcoat. I later found out this was what she wore despite the numerous occasions Mrs. Honeydew had begged her, as a good-looking girl, to wear a dress. At the girl's side hung a long, richly decorated scabbard, which reached almost to her ankles. Out of the scabbard poked the black handle of a cutlass; its worn handle suggested a lot of use. Overall, she had a rakish air and her green eyes studied *me* intently. *But who was she?*

There was silence in the room. Reluctantly, I glanced up at the Provost, who looked at me expectantly. Was I supposed to do something?

As if in exasperation, he looked enquiringly at Mrs. Honeydew, who had remained at the window.

She shrugged her ample shoulders. 'The boy doesn't seem to know anything...'

'But how canst thou be so unprepared?' asked the astounded Provost. 'Hast no one ever told thee the history of Cadaver College and...'

'Of *what* college?' I asked, suddenly finding I was capable of speech.

'Cadaver College,' said the Provost. 'Where we are now, lad. When it was founded in 681 it was called Croup College. Then in 1504, the college had a bad run of luck and money became scarce. Because of this, the College Council decided to buy headless corpses for the Anatomy Department. They were cheaper than the corpses *with* heads,' he added helpfully. 'And so we became known as Cadaver College.' He stretched thin lips into what I assumed was a smile, making him look both ghostly *and* ghastly.

A titter of laughter went around the room, which the Provost quelled with a fleeting glance at the crowd.

'But what has this got to do with *me*?' I asked, confused. 'I was on my way to school, and next thing I know I'm standing in front of black gates and there's a man shouting at me...' I had to blink rapidly. The Provost glanced away but continued in a slightly more gentle tone of voice.

'Yes, I'm sure it happened rather suddenly. But you know, we all die sometime and it's not that bad...'

'But I'm only *twelve*,' I shouted at him, finally giving way to the terror building up inside me. 'I don't *want* to be dead. I just want to go home...' My throat suddenly closed and I couldn't continue.

He patted me on the shoulder.

'The truth is, lad, there's been a curse on us here in Cadaver College, since 1010 when your ancestor Brundelwicke de Bruin was Provost. He refused to allow a known sea-witch of the time, Halbizia, to study here. Because of that,' he said, waving his arm in the direction of the crowd, 'we're *all* cursed, to return to Cadaver the moment we die.'

I must have looked as confused as I felt.

'But,' he said, 'this isn't the Cadaver College that existed when thee lived, this is a replica ghostly one. The Cadaver

College in the real world has been closed for the past five years. We still carry the witch's curse, lad, and though I've protected the college as best I can, as Brundelwicke's only surviving descendant, thou art the only one that can release us from that curse. *Thou art the only one that can kill Her.*'

'I don't care about the curse, or your college or, or...you,' I shouted at him. 'Why should I?'

He heaved a heavy sigh. 'Because, lad, whether thou like it or not, thou hast no choice. *Our fate is now thy fate.*'

'What do you mean?' I asked, curious despite myself.

'Let me explain. Due to the curse the college is sinking and even though we're ghosts, we, too, will die – cease to be. Canst thou see that the older ghosts are more faded than the younger ones?'

I looked at the crowd, and sure enough, some of them *did* look more faded. I didn't know why, but I was beginning to feel a slight twinge of guilt.

'They are disintegrating more quickly than the younger ghosts, as the curse has had longer to work on them. And,' he continued, 'it isn't just us. Halbizia sent Her hell-hounds and the Nyred to capture *thee* last night. We still don't know how thou escaped.'

A shudder of fear ran through me as I remembered their terrible baying as they attacked me before I fainted.

'I heard them,' I said, 'but what's a Nyred?'

'Another of Halbizia's servants,' said the Provost. 'Did not thou see him?'

'No,' I said, 'only the man at the gate. What does a Nyred look like?'

'He's an ugly, purple creature, hairless and vicious. The Nyreds were sea-elves originally, but Halbizia has bred viciousness into them and now uses them to do Her dirty work – Her killing. And this one – Her favourite – has often been sighted around the college. Thou art not safe from Her – even here,' he added.

With that, the Provost turned his back on me and held a muttered discussion with his Council. The jostling, heaving crowd pressed closer, sensing something was happening.

'The Porter said he didn't see the Nyred either,' announced the Provost flatly after a few minutes.

'What does that mean?' I asked.

'By now the Nyred will have reported back to Halbizia. She'll be so enraged you weren't captured we have no idea what Her reaction will be. She may draw on more of Her servants or even attack Cadaver College itself,' he said with a worried frown.

The Provost and the Council exchanged meaningful looks, while I wondered how a purple sea-elf could speak.

'This is bad, very bad', said the Provost. 'Halbizia will win for sure this time.'

Then without warning, his nose dropped off and landed on my bed. It lay there for a full minute before the Provost lunged for it and casually stuck it back in position with a sort of squelching noise.

Avoiding my eyes, he laughed in a jittery type of way, and said, 'Sorry about that, it happens all the time.' And as an afterthought he added kindly, 'Thou will get used to it.'

Several heads in the assembled crowd nodded in agreement. 'I remember the first time my head fell off,' a woman's voice said. 'I was shocked, I can tell you.'

Without realizing what was happening, my head began to nod, up and down. Up and down. In fact, I couldn't seem to stop. Mrs. Honeydew pushed her way forward from the window, and the crowd separated to let her through.

'I think, Provost, the boy has had enough.'

The Provost turned on his heel, and limped out, muttering under his breath. The crowd followed, also talking... I overheard someone say, 'He certainly doesn't look like a de Bruin, I thought they were all over six feet tall, famous warriors.' And, 'Not much of the 'ero about 'im, is there? 'e looks as if a gentle breeze would knock 'im over. We is finished for sure, and we 'as waited *so* long...' said someone else.

Mrs. Honeydew had just stopped me nodding when I glanced down to where the Provost had stood moments previously. His big toe lay on the floor.

Chapter 4

The Pirate Princess

After the last ghost had left, or more accurately, floated out through the walls, and silence had descended once more, I clambered out of bed. My leg hurt as I limped over to a mirror I'd spotted on the opposite wall. As I gazed at my reflection, I saw that my hair was as black and untidy as ever and my face thin. Yet my skin was almost white and it had a slight *see-through* quality I'd definitely never noticed before.

I limped back to bed and began to contemplate my situation. It was beginning to sink in that I was here to stay and that I'd never see my mother, or my dog, Sparky, again. Though things had changed when my father died, Mother had done the best she could and we were happy. Would I never do things with her again? I couldn't believe the life I'd lived, my entire twelve years, was in the past. I'd never live that life or be that boy again. And how would my mother cope by herself? Several fat tears slid noiselessly down my cheeks but I brushed them angrily away as I heard Mrs. Honeydew approach.

She began to draw the curtains across the high windows. 'It will soon be dark,' she said. 'Night comes in early, these winter evenings.'

I remained silent.

'Did you see that girl at the front of the crowd?' Mrs. Honeydew asked. 'The girl with the blonde hair?'

I glanced up.

'I see her *now*,' I said, 'or at least *part* of her.'

A head, shoulders and two long pigtails were emerging from the wall opposite my bed. Two arms, two legs, a body and a cutlass quickly followed. The girl floated to the end of my bed and then stared at me, hanging suspended, as if by invisible threads, several inches from the floor. I was relieved to see that, unlike some of the other ghosts, she didn't have any bits missing. In fact, she hardly looked like a ghost at all, only very slightly faded but not so much that you would really notice.

'I was just telling the boy, Fi, that you were almost the same age when you arrived and I remember *you* cried for weeks.'

'No, I *didn't*,' said the girl, her hands on her hips.

Mrs. Honeydew looked as if she were about to say something and then changed her mind.

'I'll leave you two to introduce yourselves, I have things to do,' she said, sweeping out of the room, her skirts making their, by now, familiar rustling noise.

'I'm Fi,' said the girl defiantly, her hand still resting on her hips.

'I'm Simon,' I said.

'The crybaby,' she said, with a snigger. 'I thought *you* were supposed to be a *hero*?'

'I never claimed that!' I said, stung by her harsh judgement.

'Everybody here is talking about you, Simon; they're all calling you a hero!'

'Really?' I said, interested despite myself. I'd never been the centre of attention in my entire life; people usually concentrated on everybody else while I disappeared into the background.

'So how exactly do you plan to defeat Halbizia?' Fi demanded suddenly.

'I don't intend to defeat anyone,' I said, 'because I don't intend to stay.'

The girl rolled her eyes to heaven. 'They all thought you had a master plan, but I knew you didn't. Straight off, I knew you were lily-livered.' Her hard eyes bored into me. 'Didn't you hear what old Gauntley said? You can't leave the college, because of the curse. And if you just do nothing, you'll fade away and die.'

'I thought I *had* just died!' I said.

'Dying as a *ghost*,' she said, obviously annoyed, 'is much worse than dying as a living person. When you die as a ghost, you are nothing. You cease to exist. *Finito.* Don't you know *anything*, new boy?'

'But how could I?' I spluttered. 'It's not as if I've died before and have vast experience of *how* to do it...or how to fight a witch, some old relation's enemy, for that matter.' Then something else occurred to me. 'Why are *you* such an expert?'

She hesitated fractionally. 'I've had connections with the college for centuries and I suppose it helps that I died a few hundred years ago. And I've known about Halbizia for a very long time. She's all we talk about around here. But it's much worse now, all our ghostly friends are fading and every year we see that the college has sunk a little further...we're afraid it might disappear altogether.' She grinned sheepishly at me, as if regretting her outburst. Talk about blowing hot and cold, I couldn't make her out.

'I will give you one piece of advice, Simon. *Somehow* you have to entice Halbizia into the college, that's the only way you can kill Her.'

Perhaps she was right, but I was beginning to get fed up with her advice; I never asked for it and I wasn't staying to use it. 'Why are you wearing such funny clothes?' I asked, laughing before I could stop myself. It felt really good to do something so normal.

She fixed me with a look that would've killed me if I wasn't already dead.

'*This,*' she said fiercely, 'is the uniform of Gráinne Mháille's Pirates.'

'So what?' I said. 'She was just a legend.'

For one wonderful moment, I thought she wasn't going to say anything. Her face flooded with colour and though her mouth opened and closed, nothing came out. But I should have known it was too good to last.

She floated a few inches higher, before saying in an ice-cold, brittle voice, 'Gráinne Mháille was a famous Pirate Queen, who ruled the Irish Seas, the Outer Atlantics and even Atlantis. She fought and beat almost *everyone* she ever met. And,' she hesitated, 'she was my mother.' Then to my surprise, she burst into tears and shot through the wall over my head, with the speed of a cannonball.

I wasn't sorry to see the stupid girl leave, along with her ridiculous clothes and even more ridiculous stories. Things were happening so fast I could make no sense of them, but I was certain of one thing; she was the most obnoxious girl I'd ever met. I wondered if becoming a ghost changed your personality or something. Her personality – mine was fine. Then it suddenly struck me, if that girl's mother was actually a Pirate Queen, would that then make her a Pirate Princess?

Perhaps tomorrow will be better, I thought, as I tried to sleep. Little did I know, my problems were only beginning.

Chapter 5

The Nyred and Halbizia

On the window-sill outside the new boy's room, the Nyred allowed himself a satisfied grin. How clever he was to have heard the entire conversation between Simon and the pirate brat! How Halbizia would laugh to hear they planned to kill Her in the college – as if they stood a chance of destroying so formidable a sea-witch! Did they have *any* idea of the powerful people She'd killed? For Her, killing the boy's ghost would be as simple as snapping a dry twig. After all, it was on Her orders that the de Bruin brat was now dead and in Cadaver College.

All day, the Nyred had hidden in the higher echelons of the Campanile, trying to hatch a plan that would save his skin. The Campanile, situated to one side of Front Square, was a tall, stone building with a central room at the top; it was occasionally used for ceremonial purposes by the College Council. At least now he had some information that might soften the blow when he confessed to Halbizia his failure to capture the boy's ghost the previous night. But even this might not prevent Her from killing him.

It was cold on the window-sill and the last frosts of winter still threatened. The Nyred shivered, wishing he'd been born with feathers, more than a few strands of hair (unkind people called him bald) or anything that would keep him warm. Yet despite the freezing temperature, a smile crept across his sly features, as he watched the boy tossing and turning in his bed.

Whatever his nightmares, they were nothing compared to his fate when Halbizia finally got Her claws into him.

He sighed, as if making up his mind about something, and scuttled down the side of the building, his webbed feet sticking easily to the walls. Nyreds, like their sea-elf ancestors, were happier in water, but due to Halbizia's selective breeding, they could easily move about on land. The Nyred knew he had to face Her soon, or She'd send Her hell-hounds for him; he'd witnessed their savagery too many times to doubt the sincerity of their devotion to their mistress.

All night he travelled, always keeping to the dark shadows, through fields of grass and corn at first, and later, wild moors and bogs. He avoided humans but also the local wildlife; he wasn't much bigger than a fox and he didn't want a fight with an animal protecting its territory or, worse, looking for something good to eat. The night was growing old as he crossed the mountain passes of Finea and Cuddy-Reeks until, finally, just as dawn threatened to break, he caught a glimpse of the silver ocean, sparkling through the long, waving sea grass. He stopped for a brief moment, and sniffed the salt air. It was good to be back. He missed the sea; only Halbizia could send him so far from it.

As the moment approached when the Nyred came face to face with his mistress, he trembled at the thought of Her reaction to his failure. As Her servant for over a thousand years, he knew only too well Her terrible ways. The sea-witch had no natural enemies, that is, not since She'd killed the last one, several centuries previously. Since then, Her confidence and power had grown with each passing year; She had become, if possible, even more ambitious and cruel. Humans, Nyreds, even magical creatures were there to be used and destroyed. Now constantly preying on Her mind was the boy's destruction. Naturally, She'd have Her own way in the end. It was always so.

Somewhere, deep inside him, the Nyred felt unease at the destruction of living things, but he wasn't a thinker – he was a servant and he didn't want to be a dead servant. Head bent into the wind, he hurried on. He was nearly there. He was nearly at the witch-cavern.

Halbizia preferred to be at sea, on one of Her many ships, pillaging, murdering and stealing, whether from ports or other ships, it mattered little. On the rare occasion when it was necessary, albeit for a brief period, to live on land, She sought refuge in her witch-cavern, high up in the great Cliffs of Moher, overlooking the turbulent Outer Atlantics Ocean.

As the Nyred gazed at the blue-green cliffs still in the distance, they appeared to have no foundations, rising vertically out of the crashing, white-capped waves and green spray. In the pale morning light, a misty haze shrouded the cliffs and lent them an almost magical quality. There was no doubt that Ireland was one of the most beautiful countries in the world. Even a humble servant could savour such beauty, if only for a moment.

He hurried on, but it was another hour before he cautiously crept down the slippery cliff and crawled into the cavern. A shaft of light lit up the entrance, but the rest lay in semi-darkness, as usual. It hadn't changed from when he was last here, several months ago. It was as miserable as ever: water ran down the walls, and dripped from the ceiling, green and brown fungi grew on every surface. A strong smell of stale water and rotten fish pervaded the air. The only inhabitants the Nyred could see were a colony of giant bats, hundreds of them, many as big as eagles: Halbizia's bodyguards, which, some claimed, hunted for children at night. In the early morning, they hung upside-down suspended from the roof, no doubt recovering from their exertions. The Nyred feared them, even more than Her hell-hounds.

As if by magic, Halbizia appeared in the middle of the cave. A grey hell-hound stood, at least four feet high at the shoulder, on either side of Her, hackles erect and snarling viciously.

'So here you are at last!' she screeched.

The Nyred stood shivering in front of Her, hoping that his few remaining hairs weren't plastered too closely to his head, as it didn't set off the blue-purple skin of his scalp to the best advantage. Halbizia liked Her servants to look their subservient best.

'*Greetings,*' he squawked, hurriedly kneeling. The bottom of the ocean was littered with the bones of Her servants who had forgotten to be humble in a momentary lapse of concentration. The Nyred fervently hoped he wouldn't be one of them.

Halbizia glared at him, brilliant white phosphorus sparks shooting from Her green eyes. He ducked; he knew only too well those sparks could burn through skin and bone. And Her facial tic was in overdrive, not a good sign. Apart from that, she looked just the same: neither young nor old, but terrible.

'What has kept you?' She hissed, holding his arm in a vice-like grip. 'You look like a plucked crow; a purple plucked crow.'

'Apologies, Your Immensity,' the terrified Nyred whispered, sweating that things were already going so badly. His shaking hands strayed to fix the several strands of hair, which he normally kept in place with rancid whale blubber, that threatened to break from their anchor.

'Stand still, you imbecile,' screamed Halbizia. She bent over and poked one impossibly-long, corkscrew-spiralled nail in his stomach. The long cutlass at her side, traditionally used by pirates, banged against the Nyred's head. Her clothes were a strange amalgamation: a man's trousers and shirt but made from a material that most closely resembled a fishing net. She smelled of rotten fish. A low, menacing growl began deep in the throats of Her hell-hounds, and reverberated around the cavern. They took a step closer to the shivering servant.

'Are you *alone?* Where's the boy? Where's my nemesis?' She pushed Her face very close to the Nyred's. It didn't have a very good effect on him.

'Your nem…nema…'

'Nemesis!' screeched Halbizia. 'The curse of my life! When that boy is no more I will be all powerful…I will rule the seas, the waves, but more importantly I will rule Cadaver College and those in it who tried to thwart me, all those years ago. *I never forget an insult.* So *where* is he? I've waited a thousand years for this. You should have been here with him last night!'

'There was a problem, Your Greatness…'

'A *problem*? What kind of problem?'

'Everything went according to plan, Your Magnificence, until he reached the gates.'

'So the bus hit him as you arranged and he died?'

'Yes, Your Grandness, but after that somehow…it went wrong.'

'WENT WRONG?' She screamed, a volley of sparks spraying the entire cavern and a blue magical haze hovered overhead. A hell-hound yelped and the smell of burning fur filled the air.

'I couldn't catch him in time, but the hell-hounds tasted him.' The Nyred held up a blood-soaked piece of the boy's trousers.

Her sharp talons snapped the material out of the Nyred's hand. She sniffed it and then licked the blood.

'It's his,' She hissed, 'I'd recognize the de Bruin stink anywhere.

'How did you miss him, you imbecile?' She screamed. 'You useless, purple pimple!'

The Nyred nodded miserably. 'Something was holding me back, as if there was a…a kind of protection around him. I couldn't get through it; the hell-hounds did, but only at the last minute. Then the boy fainted and the old Porter grabbed him and pulled him in through the gates. Didn't think the old boy could move so fast…'

'He moved faster than you, it seems,' spat the sea-witch.

The shaking Nyred suddenly remembered the conversation he'd overheard. 'Your Immensity, there is something…'

'A thousand years I've waited for this, a thousand years…'

With a scream of condensed hatred, She pointed Her finger at him and, paralysed with fear, the sea-elf stood rooted to the floor of the cavern, awaiting his fate.

Without warning, a stalactite, thousands of years old, crashed to the ground, splintering into hundreds of needle-sharp shards, which flew in every direction. The Nyred fell flat on his face into a pool of what he desperately hoped was seawater. He lay there sweating and shivering, but as he looked up at Halbizia standing over him, he saw Her face was a mask of pure hatred. Again She raised Her hand.

'Leave the purple one, Halbizia,' said a voice from the back of the cave. 'We may need him later.'

The Nyred was startled to hear the voice. He'd thought they were alone – who could it be? And why did they want him, a lowly servant, to survive? He couldn't believe his eyes when Halbizia lowered Her hand.

He grabbed the chance to tell Halbizia the news. 'The boy and the pirate girl, they plan to kill Your Greatness in the college.'

Halbizia threw back her head and laughed; it sounded both terrible and cruel.

'As if I'd be stupid enough to go there until the boy's ghost is dead. The college is important – more important than any of you know – but I'm not risking that. Kill the de Bruin! Use that cousin of yours, the Kyrek, if you must. Still lives in the sewers, I suppose. Fail me again, and your useless bones will join the others in Davy Jones's Locker.'

She paused for breath before continuing Her venomous speech, Her evilly contorted face only inches from Her shaking servant.

'The Sisters will be here in twelve days, for our first meeting in five hundred years. The brat must be dead before then. I promised the Sisters we'd celebrate the end of the de Bruins at our Convention.'

The Nyred didn't have to be asked to leave twice. He backed out of the cave, bowing as he did so, until it was safe to turn and run, all the while thinking of the mysterious voice.

Chapter 6

The Bookless Library

To my surprise, I slept well my first night in Cadaver College. The next morning, Mrs. Honeydew gave me porridge for breakfast. She explained that ghosts liked to eat as it made them feel 'normal'. I found that very confusing; why would you eat if you didn't need to? Mrs. Honeydew also repeatedly assured me I'd soon feel at home, even if it did take a century or two. I couldn't help wondering how homely it could be, if it took several hundred years to settle in.

Then I saw Fi floating towards me. She seemed to be in a slightly better mood than yesterday.

'Old Gauntley sent me,' she said defiantly. 'I'm to show you around the college.'

She wafted back out through the wall, and as if it were the most natural thing in the world, I followed her. Strangely, the wall put up no more resistance than if it was made of air. It was a fresh and crisp day, and I was glad to be outside exploring my new 'home', though I didn't want to be in this mad world. I desperately wanted to return to my real home but, despite myself, I was curious to see more of this ghostly place. Gazing around, my first impression was of stone-cut buildings, laid out in squares; many had stone carvings of exotic birds and grotesquely shaped beasts.

'They're the college gargoyles,' said Fi, when she saw me staring at them. 'They're nothing but trouble, always poking

their noses in where they're not wanted. They come alive…
sometimes.'

I watched as several lizard-like creatures unlocked themselves
from their positions, and scurried up the walls of the nearest
building, making for the roof.

'I've never seen anything like it in my life,' I couldn't help
saying.

'But you're not *in life* now, Simon,' said Fi, rolling her eyes,
as if I was an idiot. 'You're *in death*, so naturally you're going
to see things you never saw before. And the sooner you get
used to it the better.'

I muttered something about wishing I wasn't dead. That
really seemed to get her going.

'Your name is in The Scroll, the one the Porter had at the
gate. We're all in it. That's it. End of story! You're here and
you'll just have to make the best of it. At least you arrived in
one piece, unlike…' She hesitated, as if she'd said too much.

'Unlike who?' I asked quickly.

Fi seemed to be looking at something on one of her shoes
and then with a shrug of her shoulders, said quietly, 'Like
Gauntley told you, Halbizia hates the de Bruin family – your
family – and has tried to kill them all since Her fight with
Brundelwicke, your ancestor.'

I stared at her, willing her to continue.

She took a deep breath. 'What Gauntley didn't tell you is
that it was Halbizia who killed you! She had the Nyred drive
a bus over you. But she also killed your father, about five
years ago.'

I could feel the colour drain from my face; I felt I was falling through time and space.

Finally, I found my voice, though as I spoke I didn't recognize it; it seemed to belong to somebody else. 'So She killed both me *and* my father.' Then a thought struck me. 'I knew my father worked in a college, it just never occurred to me it was this one. I was only seven when he died and...'

'Yes, it was Cadaver,' she said, still staring intently at her shoe. 'But She also took his ghost when he tried to come back here. So She killed him twice. Or killed *and* kidnapped him, nobody knows which.'

Now I seemed to have lost my voice completely.

'Then where is he?' I finally managed, still trying to grasp the sea-witch was responsible for all my problems.

'We don't know...he could be anywhere.' Her head dropped slightly.

'Not even an idea?'

'No, and of course he could be dead...really dead.'

I don't know why, but I couldn't immediately reply.

'I'll find him,' I said, when I got my voice back. 'I'll get myself organized, in a day or two, and...I'll look for him. I won't give up; I'll never give up.'

'But you can't leave the college; didn't you hear what Gauntley said? You will die for sure because of the curse and if that doesn't get you, the hell-hounds certainly will. Halbizia will be waiting for you, now that the Nyred has seen you. He'll already have reported back to Her.' She muttered something that sounded like *the rat* under her breath.

'But why don't the Council, or whatever they are, why don't they fight Her? Why does it have to be me?' I asked.

'Because you are the *last* de Bruin! Don't you understand that yet? *Nobody else can do it.* You're all we have.'

'Right,' I said, because I couldn't think of anything else to say.

'And you understand, don't you, that this college is a *ghostly replica* of the one your father worked in when he was alive. You're in a whole new ghostly world now, Simon. There are even different types of ghosts, but I'll tell you about those some other time. Oh, and the nearby town is a ghost-town as well.'

'Is Halbizia a ghost?' I managed to ask.

'No, She's living and so are Her servants: the Nyred, Her hell-hounds and Her giant bats.' She glanced anxiously at the sky. 'We'd better get moving – come on,' she said, gliding across a large square.

And then she dropped another bombshell. 'I should also mention…our informants tell us you have eleven days to kill Her.'

'What do you mean?' I gasped. There was so much to take in, my head was spinning; Halbizia had killed me. She'd killed my father and probably his ghost. I was in a replica of a college in the real world, only this one was filled with ghosts – like me. As the last de Bruin I had to kill Halbizia and now the pirate girl was telling me that I only had eleven days to do it! And all the while, I knew my mother must be worried out of her mind. Could it get any worse?

'We've heard that the Sisters are meeting at the next full moon, and they haven't had a Convention as they call it, in five hundred years. That's in eleven days. We have to stop Her before that happens, or we never will. We have little hope as it is; however, with the combined powers of the five Sisters, we'd have absolutely none.'

She stared at me as a faint smile formed on her lips. 'The College Council is meeting today, to discuss the situation and see if the members can help you.'

It was a mystery to me what all those old, disintegrating ghosts could do, and I also wondered how Fi was so well informed. I didn't have time to worry about that now, though.

We glided through another square with tall buildings on all four sides. 'Front Square,' Fi called it, and she pointed out two interconnecting ones: Middle Square and Back Square. There were many statues surrounding Front Square, of long-dead Provosts and sturdy knights mounted on their equally sturdy steeds. 'You're related to some of those,' said Fi, airily, as we floated past. The statues were surrounded by trees and shrubs. One tree in particular caught my eye; it was situated in the centre of a grassy lawn and looked completely lifeless. Its branches were wilting and its leaves were dry and brittle. I thought that even for a ghostly college it looked out of place.

'It's called a Jalooba tree, originally from Borneo,' explained Fi, when she saw me looking at it. 'Everyone in the college is given two drops of juice every day. The juice comes from the bark of the tree; it keeps us alive. However, every year, the tree yields less and less. It's the curse on the college; it's killing the tree.'

I got the picture. It was only by killing Halbizia that the tree could live again, and produce enough juice for the ghosts; enough for their survival. I shivered, not sure if it was as a result of this latest knowledge or from the misty chill in the air.

'You don't float too badly for a newcomer,' Fi announced suddenly. 'You're getting the hang of it. Just concentrate on where you want to go and imagine you're already on the other side of walls. That will get you through them, no problem.'

'Did…did you ever bang into one or get stuck halfway through?' I asked tentatively.

'Mmm…perhaps, but it's so long ago, I don't really remember. Anyway, it will only hurt for a little while if it happens,' she said with a grin and continued to show me around the college: the buildings where the lecturers lived, and other college staff, and the empty moat which ran around the perimeter.

Finally we floated to a large building with sturdy pillars at either side. LIBRARY was printed in large, black letters over an enormous oak front door. My heart sank, as I'd never had much time for libraries – too many dusty, musty books. I wondered why she'd brought me here.

'It's a library,' said Fi, needlessly.

We glided though the solid oak door as if it wasn't even there. The sight of rows upon rows of bookshelves greeted us. There was nothing unusual about that; it was a library after all.

Though like everything else in Cadaver College, it wasn't quite normal – *most of the bookshelves were empty.*

I looked at Fi. 'I'll explain later,' she whispered.

A tall man hurriedly floated up to us. He had a long, white beard and wore a black uniform, with gold epaulettes. Gold braid ran down the side of his trousers. He wore a tricorne; I recognized it as the same type of hat that Nelson had worn at the battle of Trafalgar. Why was a librarian wearing a sailor's uniform?

'This is the Head Librarian, eh, Commodore Stanley Winterbottom,' said Fi.

Commodore Winterbottom stared down at us, a look of utter dislike on his face. 'Another student! Can't abide 'em! Nasty demandin' things. Lookin' fer books and the likes. What does they think this is, a library?'

He fell about laughing, as if he'd made the best joke in the world. He suddenly stopped, brought his face within six inches of mine, and began shouting. 'Shiver me timbers, if it ain't a de Bruin. I don't like the cut of yer jib, boy. Ever bin to sea?'

I shook my head, noticing as I did so the ships' sails hanging from the ceiling, ships' lamps swinging from empty shelves, and a large wheel suspended from the front of a 'book check-out' desk. I thought it must be the helm and, as far as I knew, it was normally used to steer a ship.

''*Tis* the only life, on the ocean wave,' said the Commodore, puffing out a chest which supported several rows of shining medals. Without warning his gravelly voice broke into a sea shanty:

Oh the Ocean is the life, is the life for me,
It's as merry a life, as any life can be.
To skim across the sea so blue,
It's enough to give one life anew.
Oh the Sea is the life for me.
Oh the Ocean is the life, is the life for me,
It really is my cup of tea.
Surrounded by these dusty books,
Now that's a life that really sucks!
Oh the Sea is the life for me.

'Is he mad?' I asked Fi.

'Almost certainly,' she whispered. 'Come on. Let's get out of here.'

Just then, a slight, petite woman, wearing steel-rimmed glasses and with her grey hair pulled back in a bun passed us, pushing a heavy trolley. It was overflowing with books, pamphlets and scrolls and her face was screwed up in concentration. She jumped when she saw us.

'I do apologize, Fi. I didn't see you,' she twittered, 'we're quite busy today,' indicating the overflowing trolley.

'This is Miss Augusta Smithering-Smythe, Simon,' said Fi.

'Please call me Augusta,' she trilled, offering me her hand. 'You must be the new boy.'

'Eh, yes,' I said, anxious now to leave – yet I couldn't until I discovered why almost all the shelves were empty.

'Are you moving to another library, eh, Augusta?' I asked.

'Dear me, no, we're *emptying* the library,' she smiled weakly, her voice shaking a little as she spoke. 'We're getting rid of all the books and documents.'

'Why is that?' I asked, curious despite myself.

'The Commodore thinks it's pr...progress. He said we're clearing the decks. Tells us every day, actually.' Glancing round, she nervously pushed her glasses back up on her nose.

'But what are you doing with them?' I asked.

The little woman hesitated. 'Destroying them,' she said finally, absent-mindedly patting the tight, grey bun that sat on the back of her head.

A booming voice came from the other side of the library. 'What's the delay, Miss S.? Don't dawdle, ship 'em out.' Augusta scuttled to carry out the Commodore's instructions, her grey skirts flying as she hastened to do his bidding.

'What was all that about?' I asked Fi, once the strange woman was out of earshot.

'The Head Librarian, or *Commodore* as he likes to be called, *hates* books and libraries.'

'Then why did he become a librarian?' I asked, mystified.

'His parents wanted him to follow in the family tradition. Although all he ever wanted to do was run away to sea. The sad thing is that he's never even *seen* the sea, let alone sailed on a ship! My father said that the years when the Commodore was alive, and working in the Cadaver library in the real world, actually *unhinged* him. The Commodore was horrible to the students, he'd never give them the books they wanted, and lots of them failed their exams because of him. He hated them, except, of course, for the occasional Geography student with an interest in Oceanography. He'd talk to them for hours.'

'What's Oceanography?' I asked.

'Oh, you know, all about the seas and oceans. For those students he even ordered in special books. My father says he's a different man when talking about the sea, quite knowledgeable, in fact. But he's determined to destroy every book in this library.'

I was taken aback by this sudden revelation; not the librarian's mad plot, but the fact that Fi had a father, and one with extensive knowledge of Cadaver College. I knew better than to pry into Fi's family history, especially with her sudden mood swings.

'Hoist the main sail,' shouted the Commodore, to nobody in particular, as he began flinging books into a trolley.

Fi continued. 'He hated the library in life and in death it's absolute torture for him to be here. He thinks that with no books, there'll be no students, not that many of them even bother to come here these days – they all know what he's like.'

'Are you landlubbers still here?' he growled, catching sight of us. He then wandered to a far corner of his domain, to stare absently at the half-empty shelves.

I began to yawn.

'I think it's time I returned you to your room,' said Fi. 'I suppose you've had enough shocks for one day. I'd hoped to introduce you to Dr. Darwin, he could be useful, and there are the geckos…I suppose you'll have to meet them sometime anyway.'

I didn't argue with her. We floated back across Front Square.

'I'll see you tomorrow, Simon,' she said as we floated up to my room. I passed easily through the wall, just as Fi said: 'You can tell us your master plan for the college's rescue then.'

That was all I wanted to hear.

Chapter 7

The Kyrek

Feeling lucky to be alive, the Nyred ran like the wind to the college by the most secret ways he knew. He arrived by nightfall and scaled the Campanile, his toes gaining purchase on the rock-face. It was his favourite hiding place, and he knew every crack and crevice in the stonework. Noiselessly, he slipped inside one of the top storey's glassless windows, and deftly caught and broke the neck of a sleeping pigeon. He'd devoured it almost before it had time to die. It was his idea of a fresh, hot meal. It was alright for the ghosts to exist on a few drops of juice and eat occasionally to feel normal, but a hungry Nyred couldn't work on an empty stomach. For centuries, wild birds had flown into college, most likely through a fissure in the college's outer walls, despite the many defensive spells the Provost had put on them. But, once in Cadaver, like a mouse in a bottle, the birds never found their way out again. The Nyred thought he was doing them a favour, a quick death as opposed to a long, lonely and hungry one. He licked his lips (the connoisseur in him could tell this particular plump pigeon was grain-fed) and decided to have a short nap before he dealt with the tricky business of how to approach his cousin Argott, the Kyrek. He dreaded the thought.

He woke refreshed, but still had no idea how to deal with his cousin. Argott was a loner and always had been, ever since he'd hatched. Kyreks are very slow breeders and female Kyreks lay only a single mottled-blue egg every fifty years or so. There was never a chance that the Kyrek was going to have any competition from family members. And that was the way he liked it. No competition, and lord of all he surveyed. He also liked to hurt things, the Nyred in particular; the Kyrek's idea of a bit of rough and tumble was to bite off an arm or sever an artery. But now, the Nyred couldn't afford to think of that, he had no option but to seek his help. Halbizia would kill him for certain if he didn't.

It was too bad for the boy the Nyred had to involve Argott. It must be wonderful *not* to have a conscience; humans were unlucky – not that many of them ever actually listened to theirs.

The Nyred scuttled across Front Square, and as he did so, he noticed the lights shining in the boy's room. He was still there then. It would be a piece of cake for Argott; he'd finish off the de Bruin brat in seconds.

A window lay slightly ajar in a downstairs lavatory. He slipped inside, a mere black fleeting shadow. Checking there was no one else around, he held his breath and dived, head-first, into the toilet – it was the fastest way to enter the college sewers.

After ten horrendous minutes of furious swimming, he finally emerged (half-drowned, and very nearly asphyxiated) from the dark, bottle-green sludge, which moved like a great, slow river of lava. A dense vapour of deadly toxic fumes hung over the sewage like a cloud over a funeral pyre. Yet none of this had any effect on his cousin. In fact, the Nyred thought Argott actually thrived on it. The sewers ran all the way underneath the college. The Nyred knew that Halbizia's curse did not extend to the college's foundations.

It was here the Kyrek lived, or as some would say, existed. His ancestors hailed from Indotica, a hot island that rested on the equator to the south; the heat from the sewage probably reminded him of home.

It didn't take long for the Nyred to find him; his enormous gunmetal-grey, tank-like bulk was stretched out asleep on a ledge overlooking the vast sea of dark green slime. His arm was protectively wrapped around his pet, a giant sewer-rat called Gobbles. The black, bloated rat never left his side. Argott looked peaceful, yet the Nyred wondered how long would that last? It was only in the gravest of circumstances that he could be prevailed upon to call on his cousin; this was his second visit.

'Argott, wake up! It's your little cuz, the Nyred,' he whispered, and frantically began to practise his most ingratiating smile. This was difficult, as fear had frozen his face muscles. For a few minutes, nothing happened; there was no indication that the Kyrek had heard him.

Without warning, Argott cracked open, in its bulbous surrounds, a sleep-encrusted eye, encased in an alligator-like head. His yellow forked tongue flicked in and out of a double row of sabre-sharp teeth. Armadillo-like plates overlapped every inch of a body not even steel could penetrate; it made him almost impossible to kill. To say he was ugly was an insult to ugly people; the Nyred knew, for a fact, even the Kyrek's own mother hadn't loved him, although on her deathbed she had admitted he was the craftiest creature she had ever encountered.

The Kyrek swivelled his enormous head in the Nyred's direction. Argott took his time, pretending not to see his cousin, though both eyes were now fully open. He sniffed the air and lazily stretched his limbs, as if he had all the time in the world. And perhaps he did; perhaps it was the Nyred who was running out of time.

'I smell fear, and as Gobbles fears nothing, then it must be coming from you, dear cousin.' He laughed in an ugly kind of way. Now closer to the Kyrek than was strictly safe, the Nyred couldn't help noticing the rotting meat stuck between his teeth.

Perhaps he *could* smell fear; the Nyred had no idea.

'Look at you, terrified...you're pathetic, a disgrace to the family; hanging around the college, at the witch's beck and call. Have you no *pride?*' He stared at the Nyred intently. 'How about I just eat you now, put you out of your misery? I could say it was a family sacrifice. I'd be the family and you the sacrifice.' Again, he laughed, his big head rocking from side to side.

The Nyred managed a lopsided smile, which he desperately hoped was ingratiating.

'It's fitting that you should come here to sacrifice yourself; I haven't eaten in several weeks. Why have you come crawling to me, cousin? Would it be the failed assignment to get the de Bruin boy for the witch? The assignment that should rightly have been mine. Now you've blown it, you're here to beg for help. Am I right so far?'

The Nyred nodded miserably.

'Why should I do anything for you? As you know, I have no enemies...'

That was true, but only because he'd killed them all.

'Speak up, what are you offering me to kill the boy's ghost?'

'My everlasting and heartfelt thanks?' said the Nyred tentatively, in a high-pitched voice.

The Kyrek snorted in disgust and then suddenly veered off the subject.

'Our mothers were sisters, though nobody would ever guess, to see a miserable specimen like you.' He fixed the Nyred with his glinting, dangerous eyes. 'Your vile purple colour must come from your father's side of the family,' he sniffed. 'Certainly not from the Kyreks. We don't *believe* in colour.'

As he spoke, thick yellow saliva dripped from the side of his mouth and quickly congealed into a yellow glue-like substance. Greasy sweat beaded his upper lip, and his forked tongue continually darted in and out of his mouth. His long, powerful and serrated tail whipped angrily from side to side, making the watching Nyred dizzy, and the ground shuddered every time it hit the floor.

'I could kill you now,' he threatened with a horrible smile; 'you're purple, but still edible, I expect.'

His enormous bulk began to move menacingly in the Nyred's direction.

'No! Wait!' screamed the sea-elf.

The alligator-like monster hesitated momentarily.

'I'll bring you all the birds I catch from the Campanile,' gasped the terrified Nyred.

The Kyrek said nothing.

'They're all grain-fed, plump and juicy. I know they're just the way you like them.'

The Kyrek pondered for a few moments and then seemed to make up his mind.

'You've survived this time, cousin. I accept your generous offer of the birds and I'll kill the boy. But you will be my creature from now on. Is that understood?'

The Nyred nodded feebly, wondering how he could possibly serve both a mistress and a master.

'When does She want it done?'

'He must die before the new moon, in eleven days.'

Chapter 8

The College Council

I didn't sleep well that night. I had too much on my mind. I was still tired the following morning as I floated into the hexagonal-shaped Council Chamber for the first time. I immediately noticed its stained-glass windows set high up in the thick walls, through which morning sunshine filtered, casting dancing, multi-coloured lights. An ornate circular table, with an intricately carved bird and leaf motif dominated the centre of the room. It was surrounded by ten wooden chairs; all but one was occupied. Dr. Gantley immediately stood up when he saw me, smiled nervously, and hobbled over. As he approached, I glanced at his face. Would his nose drop off again? It didn't, but there was something *different* about him. He definitely looked...more *balanced*. With a jolt, I realized what it was: his other ear had fallen off.

Behind his feeble frame, I sensed eight pairs of eyes boring into me. Under such heavy scrutiny, my timid smile quickly became a grimace. Gauntley indicated the empty chair and I immediately sat down.

'Before I introduce thee to the other members of the College Council, Simon, I want thee to fully understand the seriousness of our situation.'

He gave me a solemn look.

'Halbizia, the sea-witch, fought with Brundelwicke thy forebear a thousand years ago. He wouldn't allow Her come to

Cadaver as a student, so She cursed him and the college. Since then all the ghosts' essence has weakened. Thou mayest see for thyself how faded some of them are, almost transparent in some cases. The Jalooba tree is almost dead and we rely on it to keep us alive. To make things worse, the college is sinking, several inches each year. We have no idea how long this can go on, without the college disappearing, perhaps forever.'

I nodded. He was repeating what the pirate girl had told me.

The Provost hesitated; this was obviously difficult for him. 'The sea-witch hast attacked the college on numerous occasions over the centuries and killed, or carried off, many of our friends. This includes some of *thy* relations, Simon, who, like thee, came here to Cadaver after their death. Not one was successful in fighting Halbizia, though many were seasoned swordsmen and several had fought in the Crusades.'

Now he told me! This was not going well.

'Thy father, as I think Fi told thee, was also killed by Halbizia. His ghost did not return to Cadaver although we do not know why.' He was beginning to gasp, as if out of breath. He struggled on, 'However, we have our suspicions Halbizia intercepted him as he approached the college.'

So what Fi had told me was true.

'The older ghosts like myself, are feeling the curse more acutely. We are beginning to disintegrate, and running repairs, such as the one thou saw with my nose, are only temporary. We are weakening and soon will be beyond help. When this happens, the older ghosts will no longer be and the younger ones, like thee, will fall entirely into Halbizia's evil grasp... which will last for all time.'

He paused for breath, before continuing. 'Once Halbizia gains full power the college will disappear – thirteen hundred years of tradition gone forever. Thou must stop Her before She meets her Sisters. Should this happen, all hope will be extinguished. I cannot stress enough the seriousness of the situation. As the last of the de Bruins, thou art our last hope.' He gave me a long look, before continuing, 'And now, the esteemed members of the Council will introduce themselves.' The Provost wearily sat down. I thought I could actually see the chair through him, but perhaps it was my imagination.

As I looked round, I couldn't help thinking I'd rarely seen a sorrier looking bunch. A puff of wind would have blown many of them away. Gauntley was the worst. I was terrified he'd blow his nose as his entire face might disintegrate. The sight of his toe lying forlornly beside my bed still haunted me, which wasn't surprising considering it belonged to a ghost.

Directly opposite sat a man in a suit of dull grey armour, over which draped a faded red cross. His pointed black beard was neatly trimmed and he looked younger than his companions. He stood up very slowly, and stiffly, his armour making a grinding noise as he did so. I couldn't help noticing it was covered in red and brown stains. He removed his helmet with his right hand then solemnly crossed his chest with it.

'Sir Sylvester Tolkingharn-Thructon, leader of the Fifth Crusade against the Infidel, at thy service, Sire. Thou mayest call me Sir Syl.'

I stared curiously at this ghostly figure with his long-flowing ringletted hair and heavy Crusader armour. There was something else about him that caught my eye; his left sleeve flapped uselessly at his side. I wondered what kind of service he could give with only one arm.

Then with a flourish of his good arm, he executed a deep bow. That was a mistake. I guessed that crucial parts of his armour had rusted, for it was quite some time before (with much pushing and pulling from his comrades) he returned to an upright position.

'As I pointed out previously,' muttered the Provost, 'it was foolish to bring thine armour and steed from the real world...'

'A knight *cannot* function properly without his armour or his mount...' retorted Sir Syl.

'*And with them, thou cannot function at all,*' said Gauntley, shooting a withering look in his direction.

The knight made as if to bow again, caught the Provost's eye, and stiffly resumed his seat.

Next to stand in the Council Chamber, was a small, barrel-like figure, in a brown habit, a white rope tied round his middle. 'Brother Tobias,' he said, his chubby face creasing into a shy smile and extending a plump hand. Uniquely among the ghosts, he retained a tanned complexion, suggesting a life spent out of doors. Under his arm, I noticed a large, leather-bound book, entitled *The Book of Kelts*.

'Brother Tobias,' said the Provost, 'is in charge of the upkeep of our many graveyards in Cadaver College and also, of course, the hotly contested Greatest Graveyard Competition.'

Brother Tobias's face split into a wide smile. A warm colour suffused his beaming face – even the tips of his ears turned red.

'What's The Greatest Graveyard Competition?' I asked.

'Oh,' said the Provost breezily, 'in order to encourage the upkeep of the graves we have a little competition every year...I'm sure thou hast heard of The Tidy Towns Competition in the real world?'

I nodded.

'It's very like that. I call it the Graveyard Shift,' laughed Brother Tobias uproariously, slapping his ample thigh as he did so.

Someone should tell him not to laugh at his own jokes.

'Perhaps this is not the time, Tobias. We have serious business at stake,' said the Provost icily. Turning to a large man dressed in black sitting beside Brother Tobias, he said, 'I believe thou hast already met the Porter, on the night of thy arrival.'

The Porter didn't bother to stand, but concentrated instead on giving me a ferocious look.

'Thou hast the bad look o' thy father,' he said, 'the same crass-eyed, ill-looking laggard, if ever I seed one.'

'Thanks,' I said. He didn't look a lot better in daylight.

'Aye,' said the Porter, warming to his theme, 'a no-good, lazy lout, jest 'bout as useful as the Nessie monster herself and from a no-good family, that's brought only ruination to the college...'

A fat man with a bulging yellow embroidered waistcoat, plum velvet suit and dangling fob watch, enthusiastically stretched across the table to vigorously pump my hand.

'Lord Bartholomew Wintgustle,' he interjected, cutting off the Porter mid-flow. 'Delighted to make your acquaintance.' He leaned closer. 'Friends call me Gusty.' His good-humoured smile revealed a large gap between his two front teeth. 'Dashed good of a young chap like you, taking this whole thing on,' he said, waving his arm about. 'Care for a Cuban?' he said, pushing a large tin of obnoxious-looking brown cigars under my nose.

'I don't smoke,' I said.

'I say, that's dashed novel, who'd have thought it?' he puffed, not seeming to notice the smoke escaping from several unusual places; chiefly a rent in the middle of his forehead and his right ear. Fascinated, I watched the escaping tar-coloured smoke. Gusty was oblivious to it.

I tried to explain, *lots of people nowadays*...but I couldn't get a word in.

'Perhaps, a young cub like you would prefer a snifter? I have here,' he said, dramatically producing a silver hip-flask, 'a two-hundred-year-old malt whiskey.' He leaned closer and said in a conspiratorial whisper, 'The wife slipped it into my coffin as a farewell present. Dash it all, at the time I thought she was pleased to see the back of me, even laughing during my funeral. Not quite the thing...' He frowned slightly, and the fumigating smoke shot off in a different direction.

A sombre man, with a bushy, streaked-with-white beard, and dressed in a plain black suit stood up. Gusty abruptly stopped talking. The man raised his black hat. 'Pastor Colobius Longhorne, I sure am mighty pleased to make yer acquaintance, Master de Bruin. Folks call me Pilgrim, on account of ma voyage to the Colony of Maryland. Though I hears that land is now called the United States of Americay. I never did figure that would happen,' he said, shaking his head and my hand simultaneously. With a heavy sigh, he sat down.

Next to be introduced was Dr. Dodo, who scrutinized me before saying, 'Dr. Josiaph Funkelweede, at thy service.' He hesitated. 'I believe thou art an authority on dodos...' He must have seen my blank expression, because he hurried on, 'It has long been foretold of thy expertise...dodos, they art the way of the future, of the upmost importance and...'

'Thank you, Funkelweede,' said the Provost. By now, he wore something approaching relief on his battered face. The Provost had the look of a man for whom proceedings might have gone a lot worse.

'I believe thou hast met Miss Augusta Smithering-Smythe?' he said. The Assistant Librarian smiled at me absent-mindedly as she concentrated on the almost full-time occupation of preventing her glasses from sliding down her nose. She twittered hello.

'And finally,' shouted the Provost, above the steadily rising level of noise in the chamber, 'this is our student representative on the Council, Mr. Ernest Coddle.'

A young man, with long, unkempt hair was writing furiously on a stack of yellow pages. He didn't look up but continued his frantic scribble with an out-of-control quill; there was more writing on the table than on his paper.

'Er, yes,' said the Provost. 'Ernest likes to keep busy.'

I couldn't help wondering what he was scribbling.

The Provost now looked at me with a considerable amount of interest. So were all the ghosts, I realized suddenly, except Ernest, who seemed impervious to everyone and everything.

The Provost cleared his throat. 'Now that thou hast met us, Simon, we are anxious to know what thou may propose to do.'

'*Do?*' I repeated, desperately trying to think of something to say.

I suddenly had a thought. 'Where did my relation go, the one who fought Halbizia and wouldn't allow Her into the college? What did you say his name was?'

'Old Brundelwicke de Bruin? Why he is here in college of course. He does not venture beyond his rooms and he is as deaf as a post...' said the Provost frowning. 'Wouldst thou like to become acquainted with him?'

Eagerly I said yes – anything to stop them asking *me* for proposals.

'I will arrange it.' He hesitated. 'However, thou shouldst wear a raincoat.'

I was looking forward to meeting Brundelwicke – he was family after all. I was sure he'd look out for me in this mad place and give me an insight into Halbizia. I couldn't wait to meet him...it might even be like going home.

Chapter 9

Brundelwicke de Bruin

On entering my ancestor's room the next day, the first thing I noticed was the putrid smell, as if something had died and all the decomposed vapours had become trapped in this dark, fetid room. It was hot too, and I could see why, as the old servant woman who'd shown me in threw a bucket of coal on the huge fire. It hissed and spat, as the hungry flames encircled the coal to give out a fierce heat, which, combined with the smell, turned the room into a stinking hothouse.

I was already hot in the plastic raincoat Gauntley had insisted I wear, and rivulets of sweat trickled down my spine. But where was Brundelwicke, who'd begun the feud with the sea-witch and set in motion a legacy of hate that had resulted in so many deaths in my family? Including my own.

It was difficult to see as the room was shrouded in darkness, the thick, heavy curtains blocking out most of the light; only the flickering fire showed a large sitting-room, choc-a-bloc with over-stuffed armchairs and couches. They were so tightly squeezed together it didn't seem possible to navigate a path between them. Hundreds of unlit cream candles, of varying sizes, covered the delicately carved marble fireplace. A small table in the corner buckled under the weight of dozens of silver frames: each one containing a photo of a small, wizened man with a monocle and wearing academic robes. Brundelwicke, I assumed; but there was no sign of my relation.

The eruption of a loud snore startled me. It seemed to come from the depths of a large wing-chair beside the fire.

'Hello?' I shouted into the gloom.

There was no answer. I decided to investigate and began to climb over the tightly-packed furniture. After the third armchair, I found myself face to face with a shrunken, shrivelled creature, wrapped in an old dressing-gown and lying curled asleep in a corner of the armchair's cavernous depths. For a moment, I thought it was a cat. Then the snoring, interspersed by snorting, continued. So this was my famous de Bruin ancestor. I was beginning to wonder what all the fuss was about. Of all the ghosts I'd met in college, he was definitely in the worst shape; the cushion on which he was reclining was clearly visible. His skin hung in folds as if he'd been bigger at one time. And there were plenty of body parts missing; an ear, half a nose and several fingers.

I had a sudden feeling I was being watched. A pair of black beetle eyes stared up at me. He'd woken up then.

'Who are you?' he demanded, peering up at me, the flames reflecting off his monocle.

'I'm Simon de Bruin,' I said.

He uncurled slightly, and I saw that his left hand was also missing.

'Speak up, boy. Did you say *de Bruin?*' He pressed an ancient horn to his right ear.

A tidal wave of spittle washed over me. I was glad of the raincoat old Gauntley had insisted I wear – now I knew the reason. I used my sleeve to wipe my face but Brundelwicke's spit was a kind of gluey saliva and didn't come off easily. This was rapidly becoming a disaster and not the happy family reunion I'd hoped for. Not to mention the help I so desperately needed. But I couldn't give up now.

I repeated my name. His expression changed immediately.

'*Dear boy,*' he exclaimed, 'what a surprise. I'd heard you'd arrived,' he said. 'And what an escape you had from the Nyred and the hell-hounds! I've heard all about it. Yes,' he said, 'even in here,' indicating the dark room. 'So proud of you, dear boy, so proud. Us de Bruins have been a credit to this noble college for generations.'

Delighted as I was to hear he was happy, I was less pleased with the continual saliva storm breaking over me, like waves on a beach. But Brundelwicke didn't seem to notice.

'Mr. de Bruin...' I said, tentatively.

'Call me Grandda, dear boy, though technically I'm not, of course, too many generations between us for that.'

'Eh, Grandda, I really need your help. I thought you could tell me about Halbizia, make a plan maybe of how I could fight her.' Or, inspiration suddenly hitting me, 'How, we...'

He hesitated momentarily, looked confused, and said: 'Who, dear boy, is Halbizia?'

I stared at him for a moment, my heart sinking to somewhere deep in my runners. 'The sea-witch...the one you had the argument with...'

'Oh yes, are they still trying to fight Her? She's just a silly woman, and no threat to the college at all. I really don't know what the fuss is about.'

This puzzled me enormously.

'I thought the two of you were sworn enemies. After all, Halbizia put a curse on the college and now everyone is falling apart and it's sinking...'

'But that was *years* ago, dear boy, things change. People move on. I have...*I'm now dead.*'

He smiled brightly at me, as if he couldn't be happier with his life (or death). Suddenly, his lower lip dropped off but he didn't notice this, or the great river of saliva that now ran freely down his chin. How could one small ghost produce such a vast quantity? It didn't seem possible, but as I was beginning to find out, anything was possible in Cadaver College.

'Yes,' I said, 'but...'

The noise of gentle snoring rose from the chair. My illustrious ancestor wore a look of utter contentment, as if he didn't have a worry in the world. And he probably didn't, I was the one with the worries. I, thanks to him, was the one who had to fight a despotic sea-witch and save a college full of mad ghosts.

Without thinking, I kicked his chair. I immediately felt a lot better. Brundelwicke woke with a jump. I couldn't help feeling a little bit pleased.

'Who are you?' he asked, eyeing me suspiciously. And then with real enthusiasm, 'Are there patty-cakes for tea?'

I stepped aside, in the nick of time, as another avalanche of spit flew in my direction. This time, most of it missed me.

'I'm Simon,' I said, by now utterly frustrated. 'We were discussing Halbizia.'

'Talk up, boy.'

I noticed the horn was lying on the floor.

'Do you have any advice for me...about Halbizia?' I shouted.

He thought about it for a moment. 'Never give advice, boy, that's my advice.'

He chuckled to himself for several minutes, seeming to have forgotten all about me. Then he promptly fell asleep again. I was gutted. It had been a complete waste of time coming to see him. Gauntley and the others would be so disappointed. How was I going to I tell them I'd failed, *before* I'd even begun?

Something red and white, in the corner of the room, caught my eye; squinting, I realized that the candles I'd seen on the way in weren't candles at all. Instead, they were a colony of toadstools and they were everywhere: on tables, chairs and carpets. It was an infestation. I could only guess that the peculiar combination of heat and moisture in Brundelwicke's room had produced the perfect conditions for a toadstool epidemic. It was disgusting.

But there was something else I noticed now that my eyes had become accustomed to the gloom: the cobwebs hanging from the blackened chandelier no longer looked like cobwebs. With a sickening lurch of my stomach I realized the long, thin, grey strands were actually ropes of saliva that had dried and hardened in the heat. I gagged as I hurriedly clambered over the furniture, brushing against some of the creepy toadstools, so dense they were impossible to avoid.

As I finally reached the door, I had the horrible thought that spitting might be hereditary. Now, that was all I needed. And it was blindingly obvious he'd lost his marbles. One thing was absolutely certain, he'd be no help to me. I really was on my own.

Chapter 10

Sir Syl

The next morning I lay in bed trying to decide what to do and also trying to forget my visit to Brundelwicke – I couldn't think of him as 'Grandda'. His general creepiness had unnerved me. I glanced quickly in my bedside mirror. No major manifestation of saliva, not yet, at least. And hopefully never. Still, I couldn't hang around thinking about my very strange relation, so I threw down the mirror, and jumped out of bed. My leg was completely healed and Mrs. Honeydew had taken off the bandages the day before. I decided to explore the college by myself; while I knew I could never call it home, I thought I should become familiar with it, especially if I couldn't avoid fighting the sea-witch.

I skipped Mrs. Honeydew's disgusting breakfast concoction (griddled coddle kipper) or something else equally obnoxious (hake-halibut pavlova); it was an understatement to say she wasn't the best of cooks. Having safely avoided one of her revolting creations, I floated through my bedroom wall (I was getting a little bit used to the weirdness of it) when the Crusader I'd met at the College Council meeting cantered up on his clanking, armour-clad horse.

He pulled the ancient charger to an abrupt halt. Sir Syl dismounted, creaking a great deal as he did so, but to my intense relief he didn't require straightening.

'Stand, Tiberius,' he ordered his horse. Tiberius immediately galloped over to a patch of grass and began to graze. Sir Syl sighed and turned his attention to me.

'Sire, I have been looking for thee, we have much to discuss…'

'We have…?' I said nervously, eyeing the lance twirling in his hand. I wondered how he managed with only one arm.

'I've been appointed by the Provost, Dr. Gantley,' continued Sir Syl importantly, 'to continue with thy education; that is to say, teach thee the Ancient Artes as befitting a Gentleman of thy standing.'

I looked around to see if anyone else was there.

'My education?' I said. 'But I thought I was finished with all that! Surely there must be *some* advantages to being dead. And I'm also not a gentleman,' I finished lamely.

With a loud squeaking noise, Sir Syl pushed up his visor. He gave me a funny look, as if I was his favourite son or something.

'Naturally, Sire, I understand thy hesitation. When thou wast *alive,* thou learnt subjects that would help thee in *life*, and now that thou art dead, thou wilt study subjects that will help thee in *death.*'

He beamed at me, as if that explained everything. My stomach did several backflips; I couldn't believe my bad luck. I'd never liked school; I didn't see the *point* of it and it interfered with the things I was *really* interested in, such as teaching Sparky tricks, climbing the biggest trees I could find and digging for buried treasure in the off chance that I might find some. Boring schoolwork was bad enough in life but to suffer the same torture in death was an absolute insult. Death could be *so* unfair.

'Of course thou art a Gentleman,' continued the knight, smiling broadly, 'though I am a Crusader and Knight of the First Rank, we will dispense with the Arte of Warfare, Astronomy, Mathematics, Historie, etc. and concentrate on the one subject that will benefit thy education the most.'

I perked up a little. 'What's that?'

'The Arte of Poetry,' he said triumphantly. 'One should never underestimate the importance of wooing fair damsels and Poetry is perfectly suited for this noble pursuit. We won't reprise the Provost of this development,' he continued in a whisper, floating closer.

My heart sank. I'd always hated poetry, and I didn't want to woo anyone (and what a stupid word).

'I thought that sort of thing had died out,' I said desperately, 'along with the fair damsels.'

'This is a little Poem I wrote for the object of my affections,' said Sir Syl, ignoring me. 'You could learne a lot from it, Sire.'

He cleared his throat and with passionate gasping and heaving of his armoured chest read:

An Ode To Her Beautiful Blue Lips
My sweete Clarice, thy lips are as blue
As the summer sky and a Kingfisher's bottom, shriven
As dried prunes, yet it is for their beautiful hue
This lovesicke hearte must write Poetry, driven

By an ardour that will never dim, and ought
Thy glorious locks depart thy head forever, and
Reveal a pate as balde as a Coote, and a large Warte
To an unforgiving worlde; I will not desert thee, my little dove
For it is I, Sir Syl, thine own true love.

With an impressive theatrical bow, he swept off his helmet and simultaneously wiped a tear from his eye. I could only surmise that his self-penned 'Poetry' had moved him deeply. I wasn't as certain it would move anybody else, and definitely not the unfortunate object of his affections. But Sir Syl was obviously delighted with his efforts and expected me to be thrilled too.

'I don't know much about poetry, Sir Syl, or damsels for that matter,' I said finally, 'but do you think…Clarice…will like a poem about her baldness, warts, and blue lips?'

Sir Syl chuckled affectionately. 'In ordinary conversation, no Gentleman should mention these things, but in a Poem, particularly,' he blushed slightly, 'one of so high a calibre and written by a Titled Gentleman, then it is actually a *compliment* to the Lady.'

'Oh,' I said. I thought about this for a minute. 'Why is your name in the poem? Wouldn't it be better to send it anonymously?'

Sir Syl drifted a foot higher from the ground.

'Sire, I can see thou hast a lot to learn about the Arte of Poetry. But fear not, thou shall learn from an expert.'

'Your other poetry, Sir Syl, how has it worked out?' I asked cautiously.

The knight sighed heavily. 'Oh, Sire, therein lies a tale of woe, for the Ladies are somewhat confused… A previous Soliloquy on which I laboured for many months, lovingly entitled "Thy Nose Rivals That Of Betsy", was received amiss. Actually, Sire, the Lady has not spoken to me since, despite the reverence and devotion with which it was written.'

I considered this. 'Perhaps it's not so bad. Who's Betsy?'

Sir Syl looked sheepish. 'Betsy, Sire, is my favourite, black pot-bellied pig. She knows her name, and has always greeted me with a grunt and a skittish run around her sty.'

'*A pig?* And did your intended know this?'

'I think, Sire, I may have mentioned Betsy to her, once or twice,' he said, in a low voice.

I began to laugh but stopped when I noticed the tragic look on his face. A dead knight who wrote bad poetry for his intended, comparing her to a pig. It was, without doubt, the funniest thing I'd heard since my death. Still, I didn't want to hurt his feelings.

'I see Fi,' I said, waving in the general direction of the graveyards (which she'd pointed out when we visited the library). 'I think she might need me; probably something about saving the college.'

Before he could answer, I dashed off in her direction. At this moment, even Fi was better than Sir Syl and his poetry.

Chapter 11

The Greatest Graveyard Competition

I caught sight of Fi, gliding into the graveyard, its large tombstones backing onto the library's walls. I was delighted to get away from the idiotic Crusader and I had far too many problems without his stupid 'Poetry'.

I saw immediately that the graveyard was covered in that low-level, greyish mist I was now beginning to associate with Cadaver College. It hung, haze-like, over the tombstones, its tendrils trailing and hanging over the boulders, softening their silhouettes. The graveyard was divided into sections marked 'Undergraduates', 'Postgraduates' and 'Provosts'. I was still exploring when Fi rounded a corner and saw me.

'It's you,' she said. 'Have you decided on your master plan yet?' Her green eyes searched my face. I noticed she was still wearing the ridiculous pirate outfit.

'I'm working on it,' I said shortly.

'Better hurry up then, hadn't you, before She attacks us first? You've been here five days.'

'I'm not sure about attacking anyone,' I said.

She raised her eyes, a gesture of which I was growing very tired.

'I suppose you haven't any magic either?' she sneered. 'Or have you even *seen* any?'

'Course I have,' I said, as convincingly as I could manage. A magician had visited our school the previous year, and he was so awful I worked out most of his tricks. Though I didn't see any point in telling her that.

Still she must have guessed because she looked incredibly smug.

'Magic is dangerous,' she announced, 'otherwise everyone could do it.'

Before I could ask her what she meant, I heard the clatter of hooves. It was Sir Syl. And I thought I'd given him the slip.

'Sire, I wasn't finished…'

I must have looked startled, for he continued…

'I need an ally…for The Greatest Graveyard Competition…'

'I think the Provost mentioned something about it,' I said.

'Yes,' she explained, 'The Greatest Graveyard Competition is held once a year. It's in a few weeks actually. It's run and judged by Brother Tobias and the rest of the Graveyard Committee. Life is boring in college, so it's a distraction; it cheers everyone up. Like a Mardi Gras or Saint Patrick's Day, dancing all night when the winner is announced and general all-round party,' said Fi. 'Since the living Cadaver College closed there have been few new arrivals to cheer us up. And, though the college is threatened, the College Council has decided to continue with the tradition this year.'

I don't know how she did it but she always managed to make me feel like the newbie.

'We don't have the annual battle with the town anymore but it was a lot of fun. Town Versus Gown, we called it. But we had to cancel it, as some of the ghosts went wild on the night and ended up injured. Now we have The Greatest Graveyard Competition instead.'

'What's it judged on?' I asked, curious now.

'Oh, tidiness, attention to detail, boring stuff like that. The categories, as you can see, are 'Provosts', 'Crusaders' Corner', 'Postgraduates', 'Undergraduates' and 'Others'. There's fierce competition between the Provosts and the Crusaders; the Provosts usually win, helped by the fact there are more Provosts on the Graveyard Committee.

I took this on board. 'Who's on the Committee?' I asked.

'Brother Tobias, of course, the Provost, Professor Gantley, some of the older Provosts and Sir Syl. As Sir Syl is the only Crusader he's constantly under pressure, and has been lobbying for years for an extra Crusader on the Committee but, so far, Professor Gantley has stood firm.'

So that was why he wanted my help.

'Occasionally,' continued Fi, 'the Committee allows the undergraduate students to win, just to encourage them, but it doesn't happen very often as their graveyard is too scruffy. Postgrads rarely win either because they never have any money to spend on upkeep.'

I digested this. True, the undergraduate graveyard did look scruffy, as if it needed a good haircut.

'The funny thing is,' said Fi, 'undergrads and postgrads don't care about the competition, they only care about the party that goes with it. Although the Provosts and Crusaders, they care too much.'

Just then we turned a corner of the graveyard and approached Crusaders' Corner. Dozens of students marched up and down with placards. Some students supported them with placards which said 'GRAVEYARD DISPUTE ON HERE'. Others had placards which said 'UP WITH GRAVEYARDS' on one side and 'DOWN WITH GRAVEYARDS' on the other.

'The Crusaders think they have squatter's rights and don't want to let anyone else into "their graveyard". The problem is that the college graveyards are running out of room. The Crusaders have given jewels and gold they captured on Crusade to the college and think they have special rights. Yet the Graveyard Committee won't take any more bribes and the Crusaders are up in arms over it. The Committee will also no longer allow the Crusaders to bury their horses with their masters. It's in direct contravention of the graveyard rules. No doubt you'll hear more about those later.'

That's what Gauntley's caustic remark about knights not going anywhere without their chargers at the Council meeting had meant.

'Talks are on-going about moving the knights' beloved horses to a designated "Pet's Graveyard" but that's driving them mad. Some of the students are in sympathy with them, as you can see,' said Fi.

'But the placards say different things!' I said.

'That's students for you,' said Fi; 'they can't make up their minds. They're just taking the opportunity to protest about *something*. This way they can all join in. But that's not all; the Crusaders are always digging up the college.'

'What for?' I asked.

'They're looking for the Holy Grail. I mean, they have been for thousands of years. Why they should think it's actually here is anyone's guess. The latest rumour is that it's buried under the Campanile. The Provost is going mad, as he thinks it might collapse if they begin digging there. There's a fresh rumour almost every week and they all rush off and start excavating like mad.'

'Really?' I said. 'Do things like buried treasure matter when you're dead?'

'It always matters to a Crusader, whether he's dead or alive. They're a serious lot.'

I thought about this. 'You'd think that in death, everyone would be the same and wouldn't need these things.'

Fi laughed heartily. 'Not in Cadaver College. We're sticklers for the rules here. No slacking. What you were in life you are in death.'

I was trying hard to understand. 'So whatever your last standing in college, that's the graveyard you end up in. If you started in college as an undergrad but ended as a Provost, you'd be buried in the Provost's Graveyard.'

'Exactly.'

'I see,' I said, completely confused. I didn't understand why everyone wasn't buried together.

'It's handy being a ghost really,' continued Fi, 'you can look after your own grave.'

'Really?' I said.

'But what does it matter *what* your grave looks like?' I said. 'I couldn't care less about mine.'

Fi looked at me as if I had two heads.

'You haven't seen your own grave yet, have you?' she said shrewdly.

I stopped short.

'I have a grave here?' I asked, my voice suddenly shaking.

'Of course. You're dead, aren't you?' she said, matter-of-factly. 'You're in the "Others" section…with me,' she added. 'Read that as "misfits". They put you there if they don't know what else to do with you. They're a replica, of course, of your grave in the living world.'

And sure enough, just inside the gate, and next to the wall I saw:

Simon de Bruin
2001-2013
beloved son
sadly missed

I gasped and almost fainted again. Black spots swam in front of my eyes.

'*My headstone?*' I managed to say and sat down heavily on the grass. It was shocking to see my favourite football jumper draped, sad and unloved, over my grave; its rain-sodden sleeves blowing in the cold wind. How I'd loved that jumper, how I'd been so proud to wear it. No matter how many times I swallowed, the large lump in my throat wouldn't go away. I was equally shocked to see the headstone beside it; it was my fathers.

Further along, there was a much older gravestone, lichen-covered and weather-worn:

Oure Much Loved
Princess Fiain of the Islands and the Outer Atlantics
1606
Erected by
Her broken-hearted people

'So you *are* a princess,' I managed to get out.

'Daughters of queens usually are,' she said smugly. 'A Pirate Princess.'

'Eh, right,' I said. She was as unbearable as usual, but when she was alive she must have been a lot nicer as, according to her headstone, her people loved her. But it occurred to me that she could have erected the headstone herself.

To my disgust, I saw Sir Syl still following me. 'I'm sorry,' I said, 'I don't think I can help you…I'm not in the slightest bit interested in poetry and…I've zero interest in graveyards.'

He wheeled Tiberius around and cantered off on his faithful charger. I watched, in fascinated horror, as his other arm dropped off.

Chapter 12

Darwin and the Geckos

That night, I had a terrible nightmare. I was standing by my grave, my favourite jumper flapping desolately in the breeze, when Sir Syl galloped past (armless) on Tiberius shouting that his poetry should be inscribed on my tombstone. Dozens of long-haired students jumped out of my grave pulling cutlasses from beneath their gowns and began to fight him, screaming that it was their turn to win. And Brundelwicke's tiny form lay sleeping beside my grave, mumbling he wanted cake, as a large, unblinking grey rat nibbled on his toeless foot.

I woke up several times and each time the dream returned. I sensed, rather than saw, Halbizia, hovering in the background, Her evil presence poisoning my rest.

When Fi floated in the next morning, I was up and dressed; but I felt no better.

'You look awful,' she said, bluntly.

'I wasn't crying,' I said indignantly. 'I didn't sleep well.'

She cast me a sidelong glance then suddenly frowned. 'I didn't think it would begin so soon, this is only your sixth day here,' she muttered. 'Did you know that you're beginning to fall apart?'

'What?' I said.

'Look at the holes in your trousers; they've got far bigger,' she said, pointing. 'It normally starts in the ears or fingers, but sometimes it can begin with clothes.'

I stared at her, completely sickened. Was I becoming like Gauntley? I immediately felt my nose and ears. Happily, they were still where they'd always been.

'I can't be; I'm too young,' I said shortly. But when I thought about it, it didn't make sense (in a Cadaver College way). 'I mean, I've not been here long enough...'

She gave me a penetrating look.

There was something about the holes; each one was surrounded by a yellow mark. I could see that Fi was puzzled too. I rubbed the edges with my fingers, and a faint smell rose from the material. It reminded me of something but I couldn't think what. And it was important but I'd no idea why...

'What's wrong?' asked Fi.

'Nothing,' I said, 'there's nothing wrong.' But there was something very badly wrong, if only I could work out what it was.

'Let's visit Darwin and the geckos,' said Fi, suddenly. She was obviously tired of the subject.

'Okay,' I said. Anything was better than thinking I was starting to fall apart.

As we floated towards the laboratory, which Fi pointed out was beside the library, I spotted Sir Syl charging towards me, lance pointed, stirrups and reins flying. He'd obviously reattached his arm. I grabbed Fi and we ducked behind a statue. Luckily he didn't see us.

We floated up the steps, and in through the solid door. Voices came from somewhere in the darkness overhead.

'Wonder who'll win this year?'

'The Greatest Graveyard Competition, you mean? My money is on the Provosts.'

'Because they always win?'

'No, 'cause they always rig the vote. They're as mean in death as they were in life.'

Loud screeching laughter wafted down to us. Fi frowned, as we stopped to listen.

'The geckos,' she muttered, 'Cyril and Cecil – I really hate those two.'

'Who's judging this year?'

'Same old, same old.'

'Brother Tobias then…'

A young man, with wavy brown hair and wearing a white laboratory coat smiled as we floated in. Fi introduced us.

'This is Darwin, Simon, he's a famous scientist.'

'Not really,' he replied, shaking hands with me. 'How do you do, Simon? I saw you when you arrived, of course, but it's nice to become better acquainted.'

He smiled at me while tickling two lizard-like creatures that had scuttled down the walls and perched on his shoulders. Their low, flat heads made them look incredibly ugly and stupid; their odd yellowish-orange colour didn't help. But Darwin didn't seem to mind their appearance. He alternately tickled and gently stroked their scaly skin.

'Geckos,' he explained, 'from the Galapagos Islands, which are, of course, off The South Americas. I picked them up on my travels there. I preserved them in jars for some years until I died and my ghost came back to my old college. Then the geckos' ghostly selves followed me here,' he said, laughing. 'Funny little fellows, really, but we rub along together alright.'

Fi made a noise that sounded like a snort behind me.

'Yes, well, they aren't everybody's cup of tea,' said Darwin, smiling pleasantly, as he held a test-tube of blue bubbling liquid up to the light. He looked younger than many of the ghosts. Even I knew he'd written a book called *On the Origin of the Species* – though I'd no idea what it was about. The geckos, obviously bored, were running laps of the ceiling; their squeaky argumentative voices drifted down to us. I was surprised how *unsurprised* I was to hear animals talking; perhaps I'd already been at this crazy college too long.

'I blame Darwin,' said one of the geckos.

'Because of the way you look?' squeaked the other.

'No, because of the way I *should* look. If he'd selected the species properly I'd be *handsome*. Not even *gecko* girls like me! Let alone any other species…Darwin has a lot to answer for.'

Darwin bent over his test-tube laughing.

'What do you think of him, then?'

'Of who?' asked his brother.

'Of the new boy, of course! What else has happened round here in the last few centuries?'

'A bit scrawny, isn't he?'

'Mmmm…pathetic…thinks he's going to save them… Don't make me laugh…'

'How do you rate his chances?'

'I'd say no chance. He hasn't a hope. I'm surprised at the College Council…'

'Well, they are *desperate.*'

'He's little more than cannon-fodder for Her, and with the Kyrek now involved...'

His brother sighed. 'No hope at all then...'

Neither Fi nor Darwin looked at me. In fact, they were looking at anything except me.

'Those geckos, they talk such rubbish...I never believe a word they say,' began the scientist.

'Neither do I,' said Fi, 'and they should be run out of college.'

An embarrassed Darwin hurriedly asked if he could explain his work more fully another day.

Fi and I left quickly. I couldn't wait to get out of there.

Chapter 13

Princess Fi and Hildebrande

I tried not to let the geckos' comments upset me and as the days went by forgot about them. During that time I didn't see Fi, but her comments about my disintegrating state had unnerved me – not that I found any further evidence of it, despite checking several times a day in my bedroom mirror. Perhaps it was a figment of her imagination. I didn't miss her. And, of course, I had the irritating company of Sir Syl, who waylaid me every morning as I left my room. The knight then bored me the entire day, extolling the virtues of poetry and trying to teach while I steadfastly refused to learn. But today, I was determined to give him the slip: I couldn't take any more of his odes...or whatever they were.

I floated out through Mrs. Honeydew's rooms, which led onto Middle Square, while keeping a watchful eye out for Sir Syl. But I was distracted by the clashing noise of metal on something, interspersed with shouting and loud cries of exasperation. Were we under attack? Was Halbizia here for me, before I'd begun to prepare!

Hurrying as fast as possible across the statue-surrounded, cobblestoned square, I rounded a corner and came across the strangest sight: Fi hacking at a large marble statue of Sir Syl on his rearing charger. For once, I was in agreement with her, but why was she lunging and thrusting two-handed with a heavy cutlass? She continued to charge and side-step an invisible enemy, all the while shouting and screaming but moving with a graceful fluidity that was alien to me. Then, with a look of intense concentration, she renewed her attack on Sir Syl's battered statue, hacking at it with all her might.

Yet as I continued to watch her, it was her relationship with her fearsome weapon that fascinated me; they moved as if they were one. Through the constant whirring motion it was impossible to see where Fi's arm ended and the cutlass began. Released from its scabbard, it was breathtaking: its golden hilt encrusted with rubies, diamonds and emeralds, the morning sun accentuating the depths of the jewels' colours. Even I, who knew nothing about swords, could tell the blade was forged from the finest steel, its edge scimitar-sharp.

Fi must have sensed my presence, for she instinctively swung round and lunged in my direction. More by chance than skill I managed to dive out of the way. She looked furious.

'Can't you see that I'm busy, boy!' she snapped, her face flushed. Strands of blonde hair stuck to her forehead. She was panting from her exertions.

'Who are you calling boy?' I snapped back. 'We're the same age.'

She looked a bit startled to hear that.

'And why were you attacking Sir Syl's statue?' I continued. 'Even he hardly deserves that!'

She blushed. 'I like the inscription...' I drifted closer to read it:

Fortune Favours The Brave

'I like to read it when I practise,' she said, shuffling her feet.

'Oh,' I said.

Without warning, she thrust the cutlass at me. I jumped.

'Do you want to give it a try?' she asked eagerly, her eyes shining.

I tentatively took hold of the hilt, and as I did so, I felt it move beneath my fingers: *the hilt took hold of me.* I yelled and dropped the cutlass, which clattered on the cobblestones.

'You're useless,' she said, picking it up and carefully brushing it off. She handed it back to me. This time I was ready, and when the hilt gripped my hand, as if in a silent pact, I didn't drop it. It fitted, as smoothly and seamlessly, as a silk glove. I grinned and Fi, unexpectedly, grinned back. Did this mean we were making progress? That we might actually be friends?

'Good, isn't it?'

'How…?' I began.

'It's magic…the Gael Magic,' she said, gazing at the weapon with a look approaching love. 'What else could it be?'

Then something began to flow up from the sword, through my clenched hand, and into my outstretched arm. It was so wonderful it was almost impossible to describe, like a peculiar kind of energy; alive and sparkling and I suppose…magical. The cutlass then climbed into the air of its own accord and, as night follows day, my arm rose with it. It began to parry and thrust and spar with an elegance that was breathtaking; all the things I had seen Fi do only moments before. It was fantastic. Suddenly, it whirled around and chopped off Sir Syl's toes.

'It's reading my thoughts!' I shouted aloud. 'It's brilliant…it's amazing…it's…'

I looked at this very strange girl with new interest. 'Where did you get it?' I whispered.

'Hildebrande was a present. It was forged thousands of years ago, by Atlantis craftsmen in a special ceremony,' she whispered back, as if in the presence of a deity. 'They are the finest cutlass-makers in the world. Only the most important two were named, and Hildebrande is one of them. The whereabouts of the other, Halteberte, is unknown, but it's thought to no longer exist.'

'So this is Hildebrande and it was forged in Atlantis?' I said, '…not *the Lost City of Atlantis?*'

'Of course,' said Fi, nodding eagerly. 'What other Atlantis is there? Only it isn't just a city, it's an island as well. Our Legend Keepers in Atlantis told us the two swords were centuries in the making, and it has taken many more years to train them to do our bidding.' She gave me a penetrating look. 'For it isn't only mortal skills that went into them; ancient Gaelic spells, even lightning was incorporated.' She smiled and gazed fondly at Hildebrande. 'No other weapon can beat it.'

I was impressed and I must have looked it.

She laughed and tipped her nose, as if to say she wasn't going to tell me any more. It was a good story, but a pity there was no truth in it. She must think I'd believe anything! The sword *was* impressive though.

'Is Sir Syl going to teach you to duel?' she asked, innocently.

'Eh, it hasn't been decided…'

'How can you be one of those big and brave de Bruins if you don't know how to wield a cutlass?' she demanded suddenly, her smile vanishing like the sun on a chilly winter's day.

'Whoever said I *wanted*...?'

'Then again, perhaps you *like* learning poetry?' she taunted.

I blushed crimson. 'Not especially,' I mumbled.

'You could learn from me,' she said, 'after all, I'm the best swords-person in college...you'd be learning from a master.'

She really had an opinion of herself. *Master,* no less!

I thought fast; I suppose I did have to learn from someone. Sword fighting might come in handy against Halbizia...and I'd already had enough of Sir Syl's poetry to last me a lifetime (or death time). I considered telling her she wasn't the best in college, but catching sight again of the enormous weapon hanging by her side, I decided against it.

She grinned. She must have guessed I'd made up my mind.

'I'm looking forward to putting you through your paces, Simon,' she said, throwing me a wooden practice sword which I clumsily missed. Red-faced, I picked it up. Her grin became even wider; I didn't have to ask why.

'Eh, on guard,' I said uncertainly, pointing the wobbling, wooden cutlass at her. A quick flick from Hildebrande knocked it from my hand. 'By the way,' I said casually, 'who taught you to fight like that?'

She hesitated fractionally, 'My mother...in Atlantis.'

I stared at her in astonishment. She certainly had a nerve.

'Look,' I said, 'I like a good story, I really do. But can't you just tell me the truth...not utter rubbish?'

'Rubbish!' she screamed, all attempts at friendliness gone – perhaps forever. 'You're stupid and arrogant, just like the rest of the de Bruins...what do you know anyway?' Lunging in my direction, her eyes glinting with a rabid-dog look, she ran me through with Hildebrande. Only it wasn't me, I discovered to my intense relief, but my shirt. I hung there, helpless, pinned to Sir Syl's charger, several feet above the ground.

'That was your first lesson,' she shouted over her shoulder, as she walked away, leaving me hanging like a freshly butchered carcass, gently swinging from side to side in the morning breeze. 'I told you you'd learn from the master...and Hildebrande is definitely that.'

I should have known that her sudden friendliness was too good to be true.

****

Hours later, when I'd returned absolutely fuming to my room (I was finally rescued by several laughing students), I couldn't stop thinking about Fi and some of the things she'd said.

'I can't make her out,' I said to Mrs. Honeydew, when I'd told her the story. 'Sometimes she's friendly and helpful, even normal...normal in a Fi way, at any rate. Other times...' I left the sentence unfinished.

'She's a bit mixed-up, Simon,' smiled the motherly matron. 'I've been debating whether I should tell you a little of her background.' She hesitated for a moment, then sat on my bed. 'But now is as good a time as any.

'Fi,' she began, 'had a difficult childhood for all her status and wealth. She never saw much of her mother, and as for her father, now, that's another story. Of course, given her position, servants attended to her every whim, but...' She sighed. 'I don't think Fi ever had a friend when she was alive, because of who she was. A Princess is never allowed to mix with ordinary people; and definitely not a Pirate Princess. And now she's dead, she's had no one her own age until you arrived.' Mrs. Honeydew smiled gently and leaning towards me said, 'I think she's happy to have found a friend at last.'

'A friend?' I gasped. 'I've had enemies who've treated me better!'

'Oh, don't mind all that,' Mrs. Honeydew continued with a smile, 'she just wants to be like her mother. She's always practising with Gráinne's cutlass. The Pirate Queen gave it to her, that's why it's never out of her sight. I'll tell you a secret, Simon, she even sleeps with it beside her...it's dangerous and I tried to persuade her not to, but I knew I was wasting my time...she can be so determined when she sets her mind to something.' She rubbed her brow. 'The worst of it is that Fi blames herself for her mother's death.'

I stared at her.

'Fi's mother gave her Hildebrande the last time they were together. Fi thinks that if her mother had kept the cutlass, she'd still be alive. I think she's eaten up with guilt over that. And, of course, Fi herself died not long after, though from measles and not in some great battle, as she'd like everyone to believe.'

It was no wonder then she kept attacking me about my plans to kill Halbizia. And offering to show me how to fight made more sense too. 'Where's her father?' I asked, determined to find out as much as I could, while Mrs. Honeydew was in a talkative mood.

Shouts came from outside the window and the matron hurried over to investigate, muttering something about 'rowdy students'. I never got an answer to my question.

As I lay in bed that night, I couldn't help thinking that it must be awful to feel responsible for your own mother's death. Somehow, I didn't feel quite so mad at her, but I still refused to believe she was a Pirate Princess.

Chapter 14

Kyrek Attack

I thought I'd never forgive her, but the next day, I found myself floating down the laboratory steps, with Fi ahead of me; we'd paid another visit to Darwin and he'd been taken aback to hear I still hadn't formed a plan to kill the sea-witch. 'You've no time to lose, Simon,' was his parting shot. 'You've already been here eleven days. Halbizia could attack at any time.'

I felt a leaden weight in my stomach and cold sweat on my forehead. I wasn't prepared...I wasn't ready for Her.

It was difficult to believe I'd been here that long, but with his words ringing in my ears and an unfathomable guilt building up inside me, I didn't notice the streak of grey flashing past. Before I knew it, I was lying on my back with the cold, hard cobblestones biting into my back and staring into the yellow, slitted eyes of the ugliest creature I'd ever seen. Its foul, stinking breath washed over me and as I stared up at it in terror, I could clearly see bits of rotten meat stuck between its teeth, and a thick, yellow substance caking the corners of its hideous mouth.

I couldn't even scream and with its great weight on top of me I could barely breathe.

It opened wide its fearsome jaws for what I knew was my imminent death. I could do nothing but wait for the end to come. Hopefully, it wouldn't be too painful. It suddenly raced through my brain that I'd been killed for the first time so very recently.

There was a flash of blue light, like a thunderbolt, and I knew it was all over. Yet it didn't feel like the end – it didn't feel like *nothing*, which I knew my new death would be; it felt like someone was slapping me – urgently; over and over again.

'Stop hitting me,' I begged, wordlessly. But the slapping went on and on, until finally I had no choice. I opened one eye and saw Fi with a look on her face that would've stopped a clock. Groaning with pain, I closed my eye again.

'You idiot,' she shouted at me. 'You could have been killed.'

With great difficulty I managed to sit up. Everything seemed to be spinning. And then I saw it: lying parallel to me was the stinking, gigantic, unmoving body of a crocodile, or something very like it.

'What happened?' I gasped, and then from somewhere close by came a song of sorts.

Oh the Ocean is the life, is the life for me.
Soon, no more horrible Library.
To sail the waves, to feel the breeze,
Now that would put me at my ease.
Oh the Sea is the life for me.

'Who let him escape?' I asked, my head throbbing; I could have done without the Commodore's bad singing combined with the squeaking wheels of his overloaded trolley. 'Clear the decks' and 'hoist the main sail' floated back to us on the gentle morning breeze.

Fi was standing over me, her hands on her hips.

'It's the Kyrek,' said Fi, 'he lives in the college sewers. He attacked you. And...*you did absolutely nothing.*'

I stared at the enormous armour-plated body; it was at least twenty feet long. A small, grey creature darted out from beneath the cavernous frame and streaked across the square, rapidly disappearing out of sight; a rat.

'What could I have done?' I said, 'I didn't even *see* the thing before it landed on me...'

Oh the Ocean...

'Shut up,' we shouted together.

'Shiver me timbers...'

As I rolled my eyes (painfully) at the cliché, I noticed two figures hurrying across the square in our direction. It was Gusty and the Porter. I groaned inwardly.

'I say, dear boy,' said Gusty, his ears smoking, 'what a palaver.' He gazed in admiration at me. 'Knew you were a brave chappie the minute I clapped eyes on you. The fighting spirit, what ho. Don't have it myself, mind; some chaps have and some chaps haven't.' He shrugged his shoulders, as if the bravery of others was something completely beyond his comprehension.

Fi looked thunderous.

The Porter also looked pleased, but for a different reason. 'I alwus says 'e was no good, jest like 'is father afore him, a no-good laggard, a scurrilous low-down cur with feet too big fer 'is boots. A scumbag up-start...'

'That's enough,' said Gauntley's stern voice. For once, I was glad to see him, although I thought he looked dreadful; exhausted, almost haunted eyes, stared out from his grey face. The skin on his face sagged almost to his chest.

'Oh, Fi, thou didn't...'

'I had no choice, Father...'

Father? What was going on?

'But thou know that shouldn't have done it; thou promised thy mother, thou promised *me*...' His voice broke.

I turned to Fi and was horrified to see she had begun to fade, slowly at first, and then more quickly, until she looked as bad as Brundelwicke.

'Oh, child,' said Gauntley, in a stricken voice. 'Why?' he asked, desperately.

'What...?' I managed to say.

'She used the old Gael Magic,' he said, his voice barely a whisper. 'Her mother, Gráinne Mháille's magic. It is very powerful, but equally, very dangerous to the user, even an experienced user. And Fi is only a beginner...she promised...she promised me faithfully she would never use it...' His voice cracked.

After a few minutes, he visibly gathered himself.

'Thou must succeed now, Simon. She has given up everything for thee...she has given up her *death*.'

I knew what he said was true. As he uttered those terrible words I could barely make out her outline. *She'd died as a ghost because of me.* I'd never felt so bad; no one had ever sacrificed so much when I had given them so little. Now her haunting words flashed through my brain: *to die as a ghost is far worse than to die as a living person.*

I looked up at Gauntley. He was a broken man. He could have been a thousand years old.

An avalanche of guilt broke over me. True, she'd been a pain, and we hadn't got on. I hated her clothes and never believed she was a Pirate Princess or any of that stuff about her mother, but that didn't mean I wanted her *dead...really dead.*

By now, most of the college had gathered round. Ghosts were pointing and whispering; but they had eyes only for Fi, and completely ignored the enormous bloated body of the Kyrek. From the looks on their faces, they could have been attending a funeral, and in a sense they were.

I caught Gauntley's arm, which parted company with the rest of him, but I barely noticed. 'What can I do? How can I bring her back?' I implored, holding his severed limb in my hands.

'We need to talk, Simon,' he said abruptly, removing his arm from my grasp and pushing it back in place, with barely a glance at me.

I managed to stand, and the crowd parted to let us through. They were silent now, as silent as those for whom all hope has gone. I kept my eyes down; I couldn't look at them, because I knew I'd failed them all. They'd waited for years; I'd turned up but done nothing to help them. Most of all, I'd failed Fi. She didn't deserve to die or to have known a loser like me. With a sickening fear twisting my insides, I floated behind the Provost as we crossed Front Square, hanging my head in shame.

As we glided towards his rooms, I thought that even the mist in college seemed thicker and denser, as if the college itself mourned the loss of a ghost so different, so colourful compared to the rest. I shivered as I trailed, some distance behind, his small, hurrying figure. We quickly arrived at the North Tower, the oldest part of the college and I followed him up a steep, spiral staircase, with its ancient, carved hand-railing, our feet gliding over the worn stone steps.

Burning rushes, set at intervals in the walls, lit our way. Finally, the Provost turned the key in a massive oak door and we entered a large, book-lined study. Covering almost every surface was a fine layer of grey dust. A small fire burned in the old-fashioned grate. As I crossed the room, I noticed a grille in the middle of the floor. The Provost saw me staring at it.

'It is a portcullis; it protects a shaft that leads down to the college's Front Gate. In medieval times, we threw down burning oil to repel attacking invaders.' He sat wearily on a wooden chair behind a rickety desk covered in yellow-paged books, crumbling scrolls and calcified plants. He looked so frail I thought he might disintegrate before my eyes. And I was the cause of it.

He saw me looking at the plants. 'I enjoyed gardening when I was alive,' he said. I didn't know how he could sit there and discuss plants when his daughter had just been attacked. Perhaps, like me, he was hoping it hadn't actually happened.

'I didn't know you were her father,' I blurted out.

He attempted a smile but failed miserably.

'She certainly did not advertise the fact. Of course, she preferred her mother, I mean who would not? Gráinne Mháille and an old fuddy-duddy, why, even I knew there was no comparison.' He was lost in thought for a moment. 'We were an unlikely couple, a Pirate Queen and an academic, but strangely it worked. We met under unusual circumstances. Of course, Fiain is a Pirate Princess...or, at least, was one.'

I could see what a great effort the last sentence had cost him.

'When she told me she was a Princess I laughed. I didn't believe her,' I whispered, covering my face with my hands. It made me feel awful to think of it now.

'She must have liked thee...a lot. Normally she did not tell people. And she risked *everything* by using the Gael Magic...' He stopped as a single tear tracked down his withered face.

'She hinted that magic was dangerous, but I didn't know what she was talking about. Why...why was she called Fiain?' I asked in a small voice.

'It means *wild* in the Gael. Her mother thought it suited her. Even as a baby, it was clear she had a temper.' He smiled, in a watery kind of a way, at the thought. 'Her title of *Princess Fiain of the Islands and the Outer Atlantics* is an ancient one, and actually goes back to the Lost City of Atlantis.'

'Fi mentioned that,' I said, in a small voice. 'She was...she was somebody important, wasn't she? And...I'm nobody...she died for nothing,' I blurted out.

Tears flowed down my face. I felt foolish, and stupid and angry. And worse than that, I felt helpless.

'She did not die for nothing. Remember, thou art still alive and a de Bruin. Hast thou forgotten that?' he asked, his voice heavy with emotion.

Of course I hadn't forgotten it, but whatever my background, it didn't seem to matter a lot now.

'Is there any way,' I pleaded with him, 'to bring her back?'

He hesitated. 'There *is* a way, but it is full of danger. Saving the college is of the upmost importance. Halbizia could attack any day and I have a responsibility to all the Cadaver ghosts...'

'But you need *me* for that,' I said eagerly, 'I want to rescue Fi...the college will have to wait.' I fixed him with the most determined look I could muster and it seemed to work, as finally, he lowered his gaze and nodded his head slightly.

'Alright then, but thou must be as quick as thou canst. I should not really allow thee to do this because it is dangerous...thou might not survive.'

'I'll do it,' I said. 'Whatever it is...whatever it takes...I owe her that.'

'Alright, my boy, thou will have to bring back her mother. She is the only one who can fully control the Gael Magic, and only a powerful magic can help Fiain now.'

I stared at him. 'But isn't she dead, Gráinne Mháille?'

'Of course she is, hast thou not learnt anything, boy? Things are different here; the rules of the living do not apply. Halbizia was the Pirate Queen's most embittered enemy – there is a lot of history between them and I do not have time to go into it now. However, I will tell thee that Halbizia beat Gráinne by the foulest trickery, and now her ghost, along with hundreds more of Halbizia's unfortunate victims, are entombed within the pages of *The Book of Ornis*. Thou must find the Book, and quickly. And, when thou hast secured it, thou must release her and return here immediately. The Pirate Queen can help us fight Halbizia. The latest intelligence we have on the sea-witch is that the Sisters arrived a day early and they are meeting tonight at midnight. Her attack on the college is imminent.'

I tried not to feel so full of guilt. I'd done so little to help the college, but I forced myself not to think about that now.

'But what is *The Book of Ornis,* and more importantly, *where* is it?' I asked eagerly.

'It was written in Atlantis. It is a history of the people but it is also thought to have many peculiar and magical properties. As far as we can tell, thy father was the last person to have it.'

'*My father?*'

'After Gráinne was killed in the Great Battle, Halbizia wrote her into the Book. It is a period of our history, of which we know little, and the Book was lost for a time. It was found by a knight from Cadaver College, in what is now known as the Far East. The knight recognized its significance to the college, as Halbizia was by then our sworn enemy. It has been in thy family ever since, passed down from generation to generation. It was certainly in thy father's possession eight years ago, but since his death we have no knowledge of it. Because the Book was so important (though thy father did not know all its history), I think it must be in thy family home or somewhere he would have considered safe. Until now, we have had no opportunity to search for it.' He hesitated, 'I do not like to risk a ghost's life without good reason.'

I stared at him; it was definitely a problem. Still my heart rose at the thought that I might see my mother again. And I understood that I would have to risk everything to search for the Book and release the Pirate Queen.

'But how do I go home, now that I'm dead?' I asked.

'I will speak to Dr. Funkelweede. Apart from his bizarre obsession with dodos, he is an excellent chemist. I will ask him to make up his Interworld Elixir. It will send thee back to thy home, but the day *before* thy death. Thy mother will not be aware of thy imminent demise, and it is vital thou dost not tell her, however hard it may be, for time travel between worlds is difficult and fraught with many dangers. Between the worlds of the living and the dead, it can be very tricky. Very tricky indeed.' He eyed me sternly.

I promised him I wouldn't tell her. I was already imagining my mother's face; I couldn't wait to see her again. It already felt like years since I lived in Farranfoe and since *I lived.*

'Thou must find *The Book of Ornis*, open it and bring my beloved Gráinne back to Cadaver College. The others in the Book can do as they please. Thou must be quick. We have little time.'

As I floated back to my room I tried not to think about Dr. Funkelweede's brew. After all, it was difficult to have confidence in a man who thought the future lay in birds everyone knew had been extinct for hundreds of years.

Mrs. Honeydew was still up when I came in. She didn't look at me, yet I couldn't help noticing the red circles around her eyes.

Chapter 15

The Sea-Witch Convention

Halbizia stood on a slightly raised platform at one end of the dark cave. Water ran down the algae-ridden, green walls and onto the floor; the atmosphere was one of dampness and decay. The only sounds came from the squeaking and movement of thousands of giant bats overhead, giving the illusion of a living, breathing cave roof.

'Welcome, Sisters, to our Convention. It has been many years, too many years, since our last meeting.' Halbizia attempted a smile, but though Her mouth twitched at the corners, in the end She managed to look only despotic and evil.

'Greetings, Halbizia, may you live forever, Oh Your Gracious Immensity,' they chanted. All four Sisters prostrated themselves on the cold, wet floor. For Halbizia, supplication was no more than Her due.

'*Death to the de Bruins! Death!*' She screamed into the silence.

'*Death to them! Death to them!*' chanted the Sisters from their uncomfortable positions.

'It has been five hundred years since we met and I will first apprise you of the facts. The Nyred succeeded in killing the de Bruin brat, but not his ghost. The Kyrek is dead. He failed us and a servant who fails always deserves to die. The Nyred has not been seen since his cousin's demise, but when he appears, the same fate awaits him. My faithful hell-hounds,' She placed

Her hands on their ever-present enormous heads, 'reported this to me. *They* will not fail me. Between us, we will destroy him.'

Halbizia's Sisters nodded in unison.

'Secondly, one of you disobeyed my rules, the terrorizing of my territory must never be forgotten and, for that, there will be the ultimate punishment,' screeched the sea-witch.

The Sisters held their breath; they'd been caught unawares.

'You're a sorry lot,' screamed Halbizia. 'And I, the Great Halbizia, Terror of the Five Oceans and Scourge of the Seas, won't allow it. You *will* remember the old ways. You *will* obey me.'

The two hell-hounds stood with their tails erect and alert for trouble; growls reverberated deep in their throats. Some said they understood every word Halbizia uttered.

'I make the rules here,' screamed Halbizia. 'Never forget that, if you hope to live another day. You will do what I tell you, the de Bruin brat's days are numbered. Now I'll do what I should have done...I'll send the hell-hounds...they never fail...and I will send you. Let this be a warning: this is how I treat failure!'

Quick as a flash, she tossed one of Her Sisters out of the cavern's entrance. She hurtled through the spray-soaked air and smashed to the rocks hundreds of feet below. 'Now go down and retrieve her valuables,' hissed Halbizia, to Her three remaining shocked Sisters. Halbizia disappeared in a flash of blue as the three sea-witches stared down at the splattered body on the storm-washed rocks far below.

Chapter 16

The Book of Ornis and the Jester

I actually landed in our front garden (which was more overgrown than I remembered). I was amazed. Old Funkelweede had, somehow, got it right, though I tried not to think of the promise I'd made to help him with his dodo research on my return. I checked all over and, amazingly, I seemed to be intact. So far so good. The weather was dull and overcast. I guessed it was already late afternoon. I had so little time.

I was still getting used to moving my legs again when I slammed into our front door! I got the shock of my life. I couldn't believe I was so stupid, but I'd got used to floating through doors now that I was dead! My hand shook as I turned the handle, then walked into my home like a living person. The elixir wasn't long-lasting, Funkelweede had warned me. He'd insisted I return to Cadaver by midnight; if I stayed any longer I'd disappear without trace.

Putting that Cinderella notion at the back of my mind, it was good to be back, if only for a short time. I took a deep breath. I'd try to behave normally; I didn't want my mother asking awkward questions. Yet my eyes watered as the familiar smells of baking bread wafted out into the cramped hallway; it smelled of home. I clutched the front door for a few minutes, breathing heavily. I hadn't expected to feel the loss of my mother, and everything familiar to me, so acutely.

Sparky began growling and barking like a dog possessed in the kitchen. I'd never heard him so excited. As I carefully opened the door, he shot past me, knocking me to the floor. Then he jumped on my chest and bared his teeth only inches from my face. Was this the same dog I'd had since he was a six-week-old puppy? *He knew something was wrong.* Would my mother suspect as well?

Happily she didn't seem to and greeted me with her usual hug, after I'd hauled myself off the floor. I couldn't help noticing how warm (and alive) my mother felt after Mrs. Honeydew's well-meaning, but chilly, embraces. I hugged her back, longer than usual, but I don't think she noticed. And if she did, she didn't mention it. Obviously as I'd returned *before my accident* she didn't realize the terrible event that would soon take place. Sparky didn't help by continuing to growl from underneath the kitchen table.

'Had a good day at school, love?' asked my mother, blissfully unaware I'd die in the next few days.

I nodded, unable to speak.

'Isn't Thursday your day for football practice?'

I muttered something about a cancellation.

'Is something wrong?' she asked, peering at me as she chopped carrots.

'No,' I lied, my face flaming. 'Why?'

'I don't know, but you look a bit different, a little anxious. You're not catching something, are you? Mrs. Telford next door said there's a nasty flu going round.'

Of course I look different, I wanted to shout. I died since you last saw me, lived in a college full of mad ghosts, sort of made friends with a ghost Pirate Princess and now I have to rescue a ghost Pirate Queen so that her daughter could be returned from her second death.

'I'm fine,' I said, instead. Yet of course she was right, I was anxious, very anxious everything would go wrong and I wouldn't be able to find *The Book of Ornis* or rescue Fi's mother.

'Well alright, dear.'

But there was so little time; I had to see if she could help me.

'Mother, do you remember if Father had a very large old book, with a black leather cover?

She turned from the pot she was stirring on the stove with a frown; whatever was in it continued to bubble. It smelled very good. 'Why do you ask, dear?'

I muttered something about a school project. I could feel my face grow hot again. I hated telling lies. I avoided looking at her.

'I'm pretty certain he didn't. I never heard him mention one. You father was like you in a lot of ways, not a great reader,' she said with a gentle laugh. My stomach dropped with a crushing sense of disappointment. What would I do now? I'd pinned all my hopes on finding it. So had Fi's father.

'Still if he did, I expect it would be where he spent most of his spare time.'

As I raced out the back door, my mother shouted she was going to do some shopping, but that didn't stop me as I ran down the garden path. The shed was still there, sagging beneath the weight of the creepers that clung to it, and weeds choked the wooden steps. Even though my father was dead five years, it was still locked. My hand shook as I inserted the rusty key into the even rustier lock. There was some resistance at first, but then it turned with a loud click. With my heart thumping in my chest, I pushed and shoved the door; something was lying against it.

It finally gave way with a groan. The shed was much dirtier and dustier than when my father was alive; there was more mildew on the furniture and weeds grew rampantly out of cracks in the floor. Otherwise, it was just as I remembered it – except my father was no longer there. I blinked back the tears. I hadn't time for that now. I had to find *The Book of Ornis*; Fi's ghostly life depended on it. Then it suddenly hit me that I'd really left this world behind – for good.

I looked round wildly, trying to find a likely hiding place. Where would my father have hidden an old book? And did he know its value? Gauntley had thought he didn't. That might have made a difference to where he'd put it for safe-keeping. All I could see was rubbish: a couch with a broken arm lay on one side of the shed with several cracked dining-room chairs thrown on top. On the opposite side, old mattresses were piled high, with bent saucepans, torn curtains, boxes of discarded school books and my first bike balanced precariously on top; I remembered only too well the many falls and hours of perseverance before finally I'd learned to ride it. A disused pot-bellied stove looked forlorn in the centre of the shack and mildewed and mouldy papers towered several feet high on my father's desk. His black office chair was stained green, and the seat looked slightly nibbled.

As fast as I could, I overturned the furniture and household rubbish, and then rifled through the papers and desk drawers; there was nothing. It was a typical garden shed and there was nowhere else to search. I was devastated. I'd failed everyone; especially Fi and her father.

Dejectedly, I walked back to the kitchen, dragging my feet through the long grass. I couldn't help remembering the happy hours my father had spent in his shed; his only complaint had been the cold. I stopped dead in my tracks. That was it!

I ran back to the shed, unlocked it again, wrenched open the door and skidded to a halt on my knees, in front of the stove. Its handle was stiff and it was difficult to budge, but finally I managed it. There in its dark belly and nestling on a pile of old newspapers, was a large leather-bound black book: *The Book of Ornis,* I was certain of it – it *looked* ancient. As I carefully lifted it out, a cloud of thick brown dust billowed into the air. So much depended on what happened next…so many ghostly lives depended on what happened next…but I had little time and my mother could be back at any moment.

With trembling hands, I carried the Book into the kitchen. I laid it on the table, where we'd had so many family meals. Now at least I had a chance of getting Fi back.

With my heart thumping like a sledgehammer, I examined the heavy, embossed leather cover encrusted with a thick layer of dirt and dust, as if untouched for centuries. Of course, I knew the fairy tale of the maiden who'd waited for aeons to be woken, but what was inside *The Book of Ornis* – maiden or monster? What was waiting in it apart from the Pirate Queen? Old Gauntley hadn't given me details of the Book's other prisoners; Halbizia's enemies were not necessarily my friends. I grabbed a roll of kitchen-paper, and though my hands shook badly, I carefully wiped off the dirt. I quickly saw there was something inscribed on the cover in faded gold lettering. It was difficult to read:

<u>The Book of Ornis</u>

If thou art seeking treasure within
Then to open this Book be a sin
If what thou desire is fuelled by greed
Then thou can perform no fouler deed
Open me at thy peril
For what's inside be truly terrible
Intruders will find only deathe
As thou shalt realize with thy last breath
Yet if thou wish to help those in need
Then with caution thee should proceed

I wanted to help Fi, and all those in the college. I would be okay, or would I? Taking a deep breath, I grabbed the cover: I *had* to see what was inside – no matter what the result. Still, the Book put up more resistance than I anticipated. Perhaps it was sealed in some way, by dark magic or other means. I was beginning to panic as I pulled and tugged with icy fingers and a thumping heart (it felt really weird to have a heart that *did* thump again), but I finally managed to wrest it open and as I did so, I went flying backwards across the kitchen floor. When I'd scrambled to my feet I saw that the Book lay open, on the first page, but rather strangely there was no writing on it. It was completely blank. Where was Gráinne Mháille and all the people Halbizia had killed? Perhaps there was nobody in the Book; it was just a legend. Panic started to grip me. Had all this been for nothing?

I turned my back to get a glass of water (my throat had suddenly become very dry) and could have sworn I heard a deep sigh, perhaps from someone who'd remained silent for a very long time. Water forgotten, I stared again at the first page.

Suddenly, a scrawny leg shot out the Book. Covering part of the leg was a long, black boot – there were several large holes in its sole.

I jumped with shock. I don't know what I was expecting, but it certainly wasn't a chicken-thin leg flailing about in mid-air. I had a revolting thought: were there more body parts to come or was it a stand-alone leg?

'And about time too,' screeched a high, shrill voice.

An old shrivelled head popped up through the top page; a head with wild eyes and mad-looking, silver frizzy hair... a head with no teeth.

'Took yer time? Didn't ya?' said the gummy owner of two scrawny arms, emerging, like a moth from a chrysalis, pulling and heaving the rest of his skeletal body out of the Book. He clutched a black knobkerrie in his bony right hand.

'I was beginnin' to think ya was goin' ter leave me in there fer all 'ternity,' he said angrily.

I didn't know who (or what) he was, but he certainly wasn't a Pirate Queen! Now completely emerged, he sat on the side of our kitchen table, scowling and swinging his legs.

'How could I?' I said. 'I didn't know you were *in* there.' Feeling the weight of his fury, I said, my voice rising, 'Until yesterday, I didn't know there *was* a *Book of Ornis*!'

'Ya didn't *know*?' he said, incredulously, the fight escaping from him like air from a balloon.

'No,' I repeated, feeling very confused. 'And who are you, anyway?'

He began to laugh in a crackly kind of voice.

'I is the Jester. All knows me!'

I was about to say, *all except me* but thought better of it. He might know something about the Pirate Queen.

'What were you doing in there?' I asked, curiously.

He suddenly looked sheepish and a bright pink colour began to creep up his neck. He muttered something into his leather jerkin.

'I didn't catch that,' I said.

'I wasn' funny 'nouf,' he replied, his cheeks shining with the glow of a summer tomato.

'But I thought jesters *were* funny…'

'Halbizia didn't think so, that's whys She locked me up. I has some very funny jokes. Like, why did the chicken cross the road?'

'I don't know,' I said flatly. I didn't have time for this.

'Ter get ter the other side,' he laughed uproariously. Tears streamed down his cheeks, as he lay flat on his back on our kitchen table, his feet weakly kicking the air. It was rapidly becoming obvious that Halbizia might have had good reason to lock him up.

'Very good,' I said, grimacing, 'very funny. How long were you in the Book?'

'Seven hundred years…gives or takes a few years.'

He couldn't tell a joke to save his life but it did seem a bit harsh to imprison him for seven hundred years.

'What else is in there?' I asked, pointing to the Book.

He hesitated. 'Things.'

'What kind of things?' I asked impatiently.

'Things best left alone unlus ya was lookin' fer a whole lot o' trouble, and if ya don't mind my sayin', ya look too scrawny 'nd young fer that.' He stared at me more closely. 'Are ya a ghostie?' He roared with laughter again, his boots banging against the table leg.

'Only since very recently,' I said, with as much dignity as I could muster. I could only imagine that some ghostly vestiges remained though I now felt fully alive.

''Nd why does ya want ter know what's innit?' he asked suspiciously.

'A friend,' I said, 'was killed…and this is the only way to help her.'

Nothing about him suggested he could be trusted; in fact, the exact opposite. He definitely looked shifty. But what choice did I have? Fi was dead and I had to save her, the college and everyone in it. With my heart hammering in my chest, I decided to tell him everything.

'Halbizia's a bad 'un fer sure,' he said, when I'd finished. He frowned and said nothing for a few minutes, as if trying to weigh something up.

'Here's the deal, I help ya get the critters out 'o the Book 'nd ya has ter help me be funny agin. Deal?'

I knew nothing about jesters or making people laugh, but now wasn't the time to mention such minor details. Desperately hoping I was doing the right thing, we shook hands; a boy who'd become a ghost who'd become a boy again and a disastrously unfunny jester.

He looked around to check no one was listening; as if our kitchen was a haven for spies…

'They is all in there,' he said in a whisper, pointing to the Book.

'All *who?*' I asked, excitement beginning to well up inside me.

'All them what Halbizia's killed. ''Nd,' he giggled, 'they're mighty mad. Lookin' fer a chance ter get their own back on Her. Might like the hoportunity myself.' His face brightened at the thought. 'Aye, revenge is what we's want, 'nd revenge is what we's gonna git.'

'Okay,' I said, 'but how do we get them out?'

He stroked his chin. 'That ain't so easy. There's things we'se need.'

'What things?' I asked, hoping desperately they wouldn't be difficult to find and glancing hopefully round my mother's kitchen.

'Flahuvala Flowers, what only flowers for four days in April, 'nd then only in the desirt in Suth Africa. Gotta catch them just as they turn before sunrise on the seventh day of the Bolanga Festival 'nd that only happens every fifteen years or is it twenty-five?' He stroked his chin. 'That ain't the easiest thing ter do, no siree. 'Specially as they is so well guarded by Black Trolls, 'nd they be mean critters, so they is. 'Nd, ya have ter stand on yer head ter pick them. Facing east, o' course, or is it west?' He stroked his chin again.

I stared at him.

'O' course, dem Flahuvala Flowers, now they be *easy* to git compared ter the eyelash o' a Brazilian Rain Forest Choco Lukka.' He shuddered. 'I sure wouldn't want ter run into one o' dem. No sirree, not even if me granny's life depended on it...'

I slumped into an armchair, and covered my head with my hands.

'O' course there *is* another way,' said the Jester, after a few minutes.

'There is?' I whispered. I didn't think I could take much more.

'Only thing tho', it's a mite dangerous.'

I began to wonder what could possibly be more dangerous than Black Trolls or Choco Lukkas (though I hadn't a clue what they were).

'Ain't bin done too often; it's a mite tricky. In fact,' he said, scratching his head, 'I think this be the furst time.'

'What is it?' I asked impatiently. I had visions of him asking me, at the very least, to wrestle a dragon, or dance with a wild bear.

'You'll have to sing a song,' he said. 'Can ya hold a tune?'

I looked around at the familiar red and white curtains, the kitchen cupboards displaying my mother's favourite blue-and-green dinner service. Only a few short days ago, I'd lived here and known none of this.

'Only if forced...' I said.

The Jester looked at me expectantly.

I sighed, realizing I had no choice, took a deep breath, and began to sing.

Sparky began to howl.

Chapter 17

The Creatures from *The Book of Ornis*

Afterwards, I couldn't remember what I'd sung in my mother's kitchen with Sparky howling from underneath the table for all he was worth. I suspect the fact I managed at all, had a lot to do with the Jester's Black Trolls and Brazilian Rain Forest Choco Lukkas.

My singing was terrible but what walked out of the Book that afternoon was more terrible still; I gasped in mounting horror as I watched the steady march of those entombed in *The Book of Ornis*. The Jester directed them out the kitchen door and into the back garden. 'I told ya,' he whispered excitedly to me. 'I told ya it might work.'

Sparky retreated, shivering, under the stairs. I wished I could join him.

I stared in amazement at the creatures, their old-fashioned clothes, weapons and accompanying cloud of dust; they'd obviously lived in the Book for many hundreds of years. Yet even more startling were the bodies, heads, wings and legs fused together in total disarray; there was no telling what many of them had been originally: the head of a grotesque bird protruded from a human chest; a giant misshapen human head, almost cleaved in two by a bloodied axe, balanced on a dwarf torso. There was evidence of enormous teeth marks on some of the creatures and several had large body chunks missing. And I thought I'd seen *everything* in Cadaver College!

I didn't know if these abnormalities had occurred in the Book or before Halbizia had locked them in it. My stomach lurched as I realized it could have happened when I 'sang' them out.

A group of eerie, green-skinned creatures pushed past me in the small kitchen. The Jester was almost beside himself with excitement. 'Banshees,' he whispered loudly. Easily recognizable was an executioner, his black lidless eyes peering out through the holes in his hood. His powerful fist clutched the handle of an enormous axe. His unfortunate victims followed (headless) in his wake. A train of knights in clinking armour trotted out, spears at their sides, with battle-scarred hounds running closely at their heels. The last knight walked stiffly, the lance that had killed him sticking out of his side at an awkward angle. Not surprisingly, he made a careful detour around the other creatures. Several pock-faced, blond-haired giants trundled past. I guessed the ones carrying handbags were female. But I could have been wrong.

Most of the inhabitants of the Book seemed confused, as if they'd woken from a long sleep. They blinked in the daylight and rubbed their eyes.

Somewhere in the middle of the procession, a small boy ran past. He was almost normal looking, though covered from head to toe in soot. He flashed me a cheeky grin, his white teeth standing out in his blackened face. 'Thanks, Mister,' he yelled in my direction. It was the first time I'd been called *Mister*.

Finally, after what seemed like an age, the long exodus of the entombed finally came to an end. I followed the Jester outside. They were lined up, rank on rank, in military fashion, at least two hundred creatures and humans that Halbizia had killed in Her long career as a bloody murderess. Many kept their eyes downcast.

Finally the chattering, hissing, gurgling and chirping died down. The motley crew seemed to quiver with expectation, as they waited in our back garden in the autumn sunshine, soaking up the evening sun; free at last. The golden leaves from the trees dropped steadily at their feet. I don't think I'd ever seen a stranger sight, yet for some reason I couldn't help feeling sorry for them.

But worryingly, I didn't see anyone that looked in the least like a Pirate Queen, and my mother would be back at any moment. Gauntley had told me that Gráinne was unmistakeable: tall, wearing men's clothes, a shirt and baggy trousers. 'Gráinne died in battle, fighting Halbizia,' he'd explained, 'and that was her battle uniform.' I couldn't help thinking that Fi wore men's clothes too and how I'd laughed at her. I felt more ashamed than ever.

But where was she? Would she be in one piece to save Fi? And would she be *able* to save her? These questions raced through my mind as I scanned the crowd.

'Can you see her?' I asked the Jester urgently, my voice shaking slightly.

He shook his head.

A tall woman with dark tresses broke through the ranks and strode forward. She didn't look as bad as some of the others, just a few minor bites, gone here and there. She dropped an awkward curtsy. 'Master, in the world I was known as the withering-witch. I pledge thee my unwavering loyalty, my powers and my life,' she said, and flung herself at my feet.

'Get up!' I whispered urgently, not wanting the others to hear. She looked surprised, but immediately rose to her feet and made her way back to the crowd.

'If she doesn't like ya, she "withers" ya with a look. It's rumoured she's had at least nine husbands...' said the Jester.

A chant began somewhere deep in the crowd. 'Simon, Simon, Si...'

'Talk ter them,' said the Jester, pushing me forward. I could have killed him, making a speech to these released creatures wasn't part of the bargain – but I still found myself making one.

'My name is Simon...of course I'm not your master. You're all free, free to do what you want. I was killed by Halbizia...and my father...we have that in common...and now I have to kill Her.' There! I'd finally said it. I didn't want to do it. But She'd destroyed so many lives, and if I was the only one who could do it, then perhaps I had no choice.

A hissing, ugly noise rose up in the air and reverberated off the near leafless trees.

'That evil witch,' shouted a deep male voice. 'How can we return to our lives looking like this?' demanded a female one.

I hesitated.

'Halbizia is trying to destroy Cadaver College...where I...and other ghosts live since we died. I can't help you, I'm sorry.'

A roar went up. 'Kill Halbizia! Death to the witch!' For the first time since Fi died, I smiled.

'I need somebody from the Book,' I shouted, as the crowd continued to call Halbizia names.

'Who do you seek, Master?' they asked in unison.

I was a bit taken aback but desperately tried not to show it.

'The Pirate Queen, Gráinne Mháille. Do you know her? Is she here?'

'The Bookworm would know,' somebody said.

'The Bookworm?' I said. 'Which one of you is that? A teacher, maybe?' Not that I was keen on teachers, but one might be preferable to this wild-looking crowd.

Several of the creatures giggled.

'The Bookworm ain't a *person*!' said the Jester, slapping his thigh, and laughing as if at one of his own unfunny jokes.

'What is he then?' I asked.

'I'm the Bookworm,' squeaked a very small voice. I peered down but all I could see in the short grass was a tiny, wriggling worm. 'Miss Tomé, at your service.'

'But how can a Bookworm help me?' I asked, astounded. And, secretly, *How can a Bookworm talk?*

Miss Tomé raised herself to an impressive three inches. 'I don't *read* books!' she said, with a tinkling laugh. 'I *eat* the words, silly, how else would you know what's in a book? Only a complete twit would actually *read* a book. And I enjoy my work…I like nothing better than getting my teeth into some fat, juicy pages. In fact, it's been said that *I'm* the best in the business. Though I think I was the one to say it…well, no matter, it's true in any case.'

I believed her. She was tiny but relative to her diminutive size, her teeth were massive, and glinted tombstone-like in the evening light. She rubbed her elongated tummy. 'I haven't eaten since breakfast – got any books on you, good sir?' she enquired, hopefully.

'Eh, no, sorry I haven't...I could get you some, eh, Miss Tomé...'

'I prefer paper made from beech trees,' she continued; 'it's got a robust, mature flavour. But don't start me on ink! Indian ink is the only kind. Vastly superior in quality; anything else upsets my delicate digestive system. And,' I bent closer to hear her, 'I've also eaten several suspect books, written in something unmentionable!' She wrinkled her tiny nose.

I must have looked completely blank, for she quickly explained. 'I'm not one of those Vampire Bookworms, you know. I mean, I have standards,' she sniffed.

'I'm sure you do,' I said hastily. A Bookworm with standards. I had so much to learn.

But the Bookworm wasn't finished. 'I wish writers had standards. Some books are *so* badly written, the idiots who write them should be made to eat their own words.' She laughed again. 'And as for school books, writers should be made to eat their own *boring* words.'

'You went to school?' I asked, astonished.

'Of course,' she replied. 'Do you think that knowing which words are good to eat, and which aren't, just comes naturally?'

She had a point.

'I'll see what I can find,' I said. Perhaps after Miss Tomé had eaten, she'd find Gráinne Mháille. Suddenly, I wasn't so enthusiastic about meeting her...

Chapter 18

The Pirate Queen

I found a large pile of newspapers on the kitchen table, and Miss Tomé's oversized teeth rapidly began to make short work of them. As she was my best chance of locating the Pirate Queen, I didn't want to upset her with poor quality paper. To my relief, she didn't complain as she steadily chomped through the mound. It suddenly struck me how the Book creatures got their bite marks. I shivered. Outside the Book, Miss Tomé was a tiny worm but inside, she became magnified. Inside, she was a gigantic, ruthless killer.

Miss Tomé saw me staring at the Book creatures missing parts. 'I was hungry,' she confessed. 'I just ate *part* of the Book so I only ate *part* of the people in it,' as if that explained everything.

'Right,' I said, impatient now. I had no more time to waste. 'Where is she? Where's the Pirate Queen?'

She burped delicately. 'Apologies, this newspaper's a little on the fresh side.' I gave her a look. 'Over there,' she said, but as she had nothing to point *with* I didn't know who she was talking about. 'The bent old woman, with the striped, snakeskin hat.'

'It couldn't be,' I said incredulously, 'not Gráinne Mháille, she's a Pirate, she's...' Yet still I found myself walking over to her, as if drawn by an invisible force.

A wizened face looked up from underneath the brim of an oversized hat; it had an unusual zigzag pattern. Strange objects hung from it. 'Rattlesnake rattles,' barked the old woman, her piercing green eyes boring into mine.

I knew those eyes; I'd seen them somewhere before…

'What would a boy want with a Pirate Queen, even if you were able to find her?' she asked abruptly.

'I'm Simon,' I said, surprised my voice sounded shaky, '…de Bruin.'

She looked at me more closely, taking in every detail.

'Are you sure?'

'Well, of course I am…'

'De Bruins have certain characteristics, a certain look… I'm not sure you have it.'

'I'm a de Bruin,' I said, getting angry. 'And if you know anything about Gráinne Mháille, the Pirate Queen, you should tell me now because her daughter's in trouble and…'

She jumped as if bitten. 'Fiain…my Fiain,' she said, visibly shaken. 'Is she alright?'

'She was attacked by the Kyrek,' I blurted, 'and she faded. Gauntley…I mean Professor Gantley, said you're the only one who can help her now. You have to help her…please,' I implored.

For a time she didn't answer but I could see she was considering her options.

'My magic has waned since Halbizia killed and incarcerated me in that terrible Book,' she said finally, sounding much friendlier than she had only moments earlier. 'I spent a considerable amount of my powers avoiding the Bookworm. She was gigantic in there.' She smiled wanly.

Suddenly, the gnarled old woman, before my eyes, changed into someone younger, someone in command: a Pirate Queen. She wore dark trousers, a white shirt, red waistcoat and a cutlass hung at her side. A yellow scarf covered most of her black, streaked-with-grey hair. She looked remarkably like Fi.

'You must be a friend,' she said, 'only a friend could open *The Book of Ornis,* and I thank you, from the bottom of my heart, for what you have done for me, and my daughter.'

I nodded, more or less, speechless. It was my first encounter with a Pirate Queen and I wasn't certain of protocol.

'How much time do you have?' she asked.

'A few hours,' I said, 'I have to be back in Cadaver by midnight, or I'll die too.' My hand closed around the thin phial of Interworld Elixir Dr. Dodo had given me for my return journey. But to my horror it wasn't in my pocket. Had I lost it?

'I'll try to be ready,' said the Pirate Queen. 'I should have recovered enough of my strength to go with you. I hope', her forehead creased into a worried frown, 'it won't be too late to help Fiain. You must be very good friends', she continued, 'to have risked your own life to come here.'

That was a tricky one; I didn't know how to tell her Fi had almost died as a ghost because of me. She must have sensed this, because she asked about Hildebrande.

'She practises with it all the time,' I said.

The Pirate Queen smiled. 'It's very valuable, apart from its power. Each stone represents a famous family victory. It forms part of the family Treasure; our family are not new to the pirate business,' she laughed.

Out of the corner of my eye I saw the Jester trying to catch my attention. I excused myself and hurried over to him.

'Have you got the phial?' I asked anxiously.

'A nail file is no good,' he said, looking askance, 'ya will never kill the witch with it.'

'Oh…never mind, I must have left it in the kitchen. My mother isn't back, is she?' I glanced at the crowd who seemed a bit restless. 'I hope the neighbours won't complain, call the police or something…'

'No,' he said, 'she ain't 'nd don't worry about those,' waving a skinny arm in the Book creatures' direction. 'But we'se are wasting time. Ya should be gettin' ready to face Halbizia. She won't be pleased to hears we'se are out o' the Book.' And then, rather suddenly, asked, 'What are yer talents?'

'Talents?' I asked, mystified.

'Duellin', sorcery, wild-boar spearin'?'

'What's wild boar-spearing got to do with anything? Or sorcery?' I said.

'If ya could fight a wild boar, ya might stand a small chance against the witch. And if ya knew about sorcery,' he hesitated, 'ya could sorcerer Her, or somethin'…'

I shook my head.

'I have it!' he said excitedly. 'We'se'll find ya a wild boar.'

He really was something else.

'Afraid, are ya? Thought the de Bruins weren't afraid of nothin'!'

'So I've heard,' I replied, unable to avoid a note of sarcasm.

'I knows,' he continued, 'the northern Germanica forests. Before I died we'se were hunting boar there. Massive hairy beasts, four feet at the shoulder with six feet tusks. Oh, the fun we'se had, with staves and on foot.' He looked momentarily happy. 'There's no time ter lose, we'se should go now.'

'But we have to get back,' I said weakly, 'Fi and the Pirate Queen...' I looked at Gráinne anxiously, but she'd fallen asleep, sitting on the grass in the sunlight, her back resting against a tree.

There was a blinding flash of green light and I could feel myself falling. From a distance, I could hear the Jester laughing like a madman.

Moments later, I was lying face down. There was a strong smell of earth and leaves.

'It worked,' shouted the Jester, jumping up and down beside me. 'I'se didn't think it would, but it did!'

I felt as if I'd been stuck with a million tiny daggers and slowly worked my way into a sitting position. We were in a small clearing, and the light was thin and strained as if filtered through densely packed tree-trunks and leaves before reaching its final destination. It was a forest and it felt like a very old one.

To my right, a deafening squeal of rage erupted from the trees, just feet away. A pair of small, piggy eyes, encased in a head of black bristles and dense bone, charged in my direction. Two yellow, impaling tusks thundered towards me, aimed at my midriff. At the last possible second, the Jester pushed me into nearby bushes as the full-grown boar thundered past in a vicious blur, missing me by inches. His terrifying squeals rent the air as he disappeared into the waiting forest, flattening everything in his path. I held my breath. The air shimmered where he'd passed.

'A Germanica forest boar,' announced the Jester. 'What an honour to sees so magnificent a beast, we'se so lucky...'

'Lucky?' I roared at him. 'Is that what you'd call it? He almost speared me with those tusks!'

But the stricken look on the Jester's face made me stop. 'I have to get back,' I said, 'I haven't time for this...'

There was disappointment in his eyes. I suppose he thought I wasn't fit to be a de Bruin either, or, like Gráinne, didn't think I even was one!

The Jester walked to the top of a nearby hill, all the while muttering and shaking his head that, 'The de Bruin couldn't even kill a piglet.'

Shaking from the shock of my near miss with a full-grown, wild (in every sense) boar, I followed him. There was another flash of green light and we tumbled onto the grass in my back garden.

'Had an adventure?' asked the Pirate Queen, wide awake and taking everything in. 'The night draws near and we should make preparations for our journey.'

'So soon?' I managed to say. With a sickening lurch of my stomach, I realized I still hadn't found the phial or spent time with my mother.

Suddenly we were surrounded by all the grotesque creatures from the Book. 'Please, Sire, take us with you?' begged a particularly startling woman with two heads, both sets of lips moving simultaneously. I didn't know which set to look at.

She unnerved me, as did all the others crowding around. They began to chant, 'Please take us. Please take us.'

'They have suffered too,' said the Pirate Queen. 'I shall use my powers to take them with me.'

A great cheer rang out from the crowd. They were happy at least.

'We will leave immediately,' she said, 'it grows late.' And, in a flash of blue they'd disappeared. She'd taken the Jester too, *The Book of Ornis* clenched under one arm. I wasn't sorry to see him go but now I was alone.

As the flash died away, I hurried inside. The phial wasn't on the table or the kitchen counters. Then where was it? I tried to stem my rising panic. I rushed out to the garden shed, but what hope would I have of finding it in all the rubbish? I searched as best I could – but it wasn't there. Then it hit me: Sparky. I raced back to the kitchen and discovered him under the couch, chewing contentedly. He tried to wriggle away as I prised something from between his now-clenched jaws – it was the phial, but it was covered in teeth marks, and most of the Interworld Elixir had leaked out. Still, maybe there was enough left to return me to Cadaver in one piece. I desperately hoped so, as Gauntley had warned me the Interworld Elixir was the only way I could go back.

The kitchen door opened and in walked my mother, weighed down with shopping bags. I rushed to help her. She seemed surprised but didn't comment. Then came the awful moment I'd been dreading all day.

'I have to go...to bed,' I said abruptly.

'Isn't it a little early, dear?' she said anxiously, glancing at the clock. 'It's not...'

'Goodnight...' I said escaping up the stairs, two steps at a time, trying not to cry.

'Let's do something nice at the weekend,' she called after me. 'You decide this time.'

Little did she know I'd soon be killed by Halbizia. The unfairness of it made me angry all over again.

Back in my bedroom, with my old football boots hanging behind the door, and my favourite soccer posters on the walls, I swallowed the remaining Interworld Elixir and a minute later landed in Front Square.

Chapter 19

The Return of Fi

I didn't see what the Pirate Queen did to restore Fi to her ghostly self. It was a private affair between mother and daughter, and took place in Gauntley's rooms. It was a pity; I wanted to see and practise more of the Gael Magic. I had a feeling it could come in useful.

The day after we returned to Cadaver, the Pirate Princess floated out to Front Square, as if nothing had happened. She looked happy to be back but when I tried to thank her (rather awkwardly admittedly) for having saved me from the Kyrek, she just laughed. 'Let's face it, you need somebody to save you, Simon.' Then she grew more serious. 'Although *thank you* for rescuing my mother, so she could save me. Um…sorry for hanging you up like that. We could continue your lessons if you like?'

'Okay, how about we call it quits?' I said, laughing, and holding out my hand.

'Quits,' she replied, smiling, as she shook it.

I sensed she didn't want to talk about her ghostly death and I decided not to ask about it. That didn't, however, stop her from laughing hysterically every time the Germanica boar incident was mentioned. 'All college is talking about it,' she giggled. 'It's the best entertainment we've had in years. That Jester is quite a character, isn't he?'

I could think of other things to call him. But the Jester was pushed out of my mind as we practised more duelling (I was getting slightly better) and she also showed me how to perform a sleeping charm – tickle the person on their nose and say 'Slumberate' as many times as it took to work.

I felt such an idiot shouting, 'Slumberate!'

'You need more practice,' said Fi, not caring one whit for my feelings.

Happily, Gauntley's voice boomed out across the square. He'd called a meeting of the entire college in front of the library. The Pirate Queen stood on the steps to his right, proud and wild looking, but from my position at the front of the crowd, I thought she looked tired when she smiled at her husband. The College Council flanked the Provost to his left. Miss Smithering-Smythe must have thought it was fancy-dress, judging by her strange purple outfit. The black, feather boa around her neck seemed to be in danger of strangling her and she had what closely resembled a stuffed cat balanced, at a terrifying angle, on her head. I'd never seen her in anything other than her grey skirt and tweeds. She looked very uncomfortable – I sensed she regretted her unusual choice of outfit.

'Welcome one, welcome all,' shouted the Provost, his smile almost splitting his face in two. He was a new ghost. The years had fallen away and he didn't look a day over two hundred.

A great round of applause burst forth from the crowd; the college's inhabitants were there to a ghost and they'd caught the Provost's jubilant mood. It was clear they saw this as a great occasion as all wore their best clothes. The women sported gaily-coloured parasols and dresses; and for the men, top hats and richly embroidered waistcoats were much in evidence. Even the monks and students had made an effort (several of the latter had even combed their hair – a minor miracle in itself). Luckily, Mrs. Honeydew had found me a black academic gown, as my jeans were in tatters. It smelled rather unpleasantly of fish.

The ghosts chattered excitedly to each other, pointing out the Pirate Queen, Fi and occasionally me. To my left, and standing back from the main crowd, I saw the Jester and some of the other creatures from the Book. They'd made it back in one piece – relatively speaking, of course, as most of them were already *in* pieces or without pieces, thanks to the Bookworm.

'To start us off,' said Gauntley, 'I think it would be appropriate to celebrate the safe return of my beloved daughter,' (he gazed lovingly at Fi) 'my wife,' (turning to the Pirate Queen and smiling warmly) 'and this young man, Simon. He has only been with us a few weeks; nevertheless, he has already proved himself a true de Bruin hero. Thee hast given us hope, where none previously existed,' he said, looking at me. 'My humble thanks for returning my family.'

I blushed and stared at the ground.

A great round of applause rang out. For some reason, I felt a lump in my throat and I had to swallow several times to get rid of it.

Gauntley held up his hand and finally the excited crowd grew quiet.

'I cannot tell thee how happy I am to see my dear wife again, after so many years.' The Pirate Queen smiled at the crowd, and Fi, I couldn't help notice, looked immensely proud too. 'But, alas, we are soon to part, as we have had word her territory is under attack.' His hands shook slightly as he lifted *The Book of Ornis*. 'As thou wilt have realized, this is both a sad and happy day. I also want to welcome the people entombed in this book by Halbizia.'

Everyone cheered again, but not quite so loudly. The creatures from the Book hung back on the edge of the crowd, unsure, until now, of their welcome. And, perhaps, still not *that* sure.

'And now,' shouted Gauntley, recovering somewhat, 'we'll have a Feast to celebrate the return of our friends and to welcome our new ones.'

The ghosts moved, en masse, towards an enormous circular table. As they did so, I couldn't help thinking what a mad-looking bunch they were.

'Plenty of crazy characters in this college,' said Fi, as if reading my mind.

'Why is that?' I asked, deeply interested, as we followed the crowd. Brother Tobias was already busily passing around glasses of mead, which he'd brewed himself.

'Dunno. Maybe they don't get out enough or, should I say, they don't get out at all, which leads to cabin-fever. But I think that Cadaver College, when it was full of humans and not their ghosts, always attracted eccentric types.'

'Why?' I asked.

'When a real college it was located on the east coast of Ireland, in Dublin, actually. Students came here from all over,

Eurasia, the Americas and even the Outer Atlantics. And some of them were definitely odd, and that seemed to attract even more weird and wacky types. That included the staff, lecturers and Provosts.'

'At least they're not boring,' I said, taking in their general eccentricity.

'They're definitely not that,' said Fi laughing, 'yet, as we're locked in here, that's probably a good thing...unless you kill Halbizia.'

I hadn't thought of that, but it certainly made sense. And if I could pull it off, I'd be able to find my father. I felt that familiar lump in my throat but I wouldn't think about that now. Tonight was a night for enjoyment. Almost all the ghosts were seated at the enormous circular table before Fi and I found a place. I later found out why it was round.

Chapter 20

The Feast

As a setting for the Feast it was perfect; the backdrop of old college buildings sheltered us from the evening breeze and tiny red and orange lights winked prettily from the low-lying shrubs and college statues. The air was filled with the delicious smells of cooking and one of the branches of the Jalooba tree drooped over where we sat; its perfume wafted over us. Fi told me it had a similar smell to lilac in the living world.

On a night like this it was difficult to imagine there was someone out there who wanted to kill us…kill me. Halbizia had already succeeded in a way, I suppose, as I was actually dead but it hadn't been the end. Luckily for me, there was life as a ghost.

A plate piled high with turkey was placed before each ghost, but before my very eyes the plate moved! 'It's a rotating table,' explained Fi, laughing as she did so. As the circular table spun round, I soon lost sight of my dinner. After ten minutes or so, it reappeared and I managed to take a few bites of my turkey leg. I'd ask somebody about this strange system later.

While the table was undoubtedly a mystery, the food was delicious. The college servants had surpassed themselves; not even when alive did I experience anything like the Feast that unfolded before me. There were mounds of juicy steaks, fat roast chickens and tasty mushroom pies; these were surrounded by crispy baked potatoes. Platters of steaming vegetables filled the centre of the table and the rich gravy was the most delicious I'd ever eaten. The ghosts attacked the Feast with gusto and, for dessert, there was a luscious lemon meringue pie that melted in my mouth. Its crisp pastry, lemony filling and sweet meringue topping was magical and slipped down like a dream. Next, we had toffee ice-cream, chocolate éclairs, raspberry pots, blueberry muffins and fresh strawberries.

My enjoyment of the food was only slightly marred by Dr. Funkelweede, who, due to unfortunate seating arrangements, sat beside me. Never one to miss a good opportunity, he droned *ad nauseum* about dodos, making even the delicious blueberry muffins difficult to enjoy. 'My sources tell me there have been sightings on almost every continent. It's clear,' he continued, 'that with targeted, in-depth research many uses would quickly be revealed for this most noble of birds,' he said happily, downing a chocolate éclair in one bite, and smacking his almost transparent lips approvingly. Reaching for his fourth, he confided in an urgent whisper, 'I'm going to train them to fly...'

I must have looked as amazed as I felt, for he continued, 'Yes, I know, it's an unusual approach, but I think for that reason alone it will work...' He munched his éclair appreciatively (having first noisily sucked the cream from one end), a happy smile playing on his lips. 'It's simply the case that nobody has tried...'

'Have one of these,' I said, grabbing a plate of lavender-scented macaroons, 'I think you might like them, sir...have three...they're small...'

'Thank you, my boy, very thoughtful...lavender...hmm...a very versatile herb with great antiseptic properties. Now, where was I? Yes, if we can pull it off, and train them to fly, it will put Cadaver College at the forefront of academic research...cutting edge, don't you know, as we academics like to say.' His smile widened as his blue-tinged hand reached for the last éclair, content in the knowledge he was on the right track.

In despair, I turned to Fi, and said the first thing that popped into my head. 'I miss my mother. I'm getting used to it here but it's still hard being away from her. I saw her...only for a few minutes though.'

I expected her to laugh but she didn't. 'If you kill Halbizia, perhaps you could return to her,' she said seriously. 'There are six types of ghosts: Earthwalkers, Zombies, Grey Ghosts, Lifers, Revived Corpses and Other Shades and Spooks. With Halbizia dead, you could return to the living world, and your mother, as an Earthwalker. Actually, you're probably already in that category because you returned for a day.'

This was really news.

'Then if I kill the witch I might be able to go home?'

Fi nodded and slyly added, 'If you attended lessons you could find out more about Earthwalkers and the other categories.'

I let that pass. Clearly, she was in a talking mood so I decided to ask her a question. 'What would you like to have done, you know, if you'd lived and grown up?'

She hesitated only slightly. 'My mother would have expected me to join the family business, become a pirate.' She glanced at the Pirate Queen beside her, deep in conversation with her father. 'I might anyway, but a ghostly one of course, if we ever manage to leave here.' Then changing the subject, she said, 'I'll tell you something scandalous. Miss Smithering-Smythe was a suffragette...she fought for women's rights. You wouldn't think it to look at her, would you?'

I actually couldn't imagine anyone *less* like a suffragette. However, her next comment was a complete bombshell.

'I overheard my father telling Sir Syl that you'll soon begin your real education here. He doesn't want to wait any longer, and certainly,' she began to laugh again, 'when he heard about the wild boar disaster...'

'What?' I said. 'You can't be serious. I don't want...'

'That's obvious,' she giggled, 'but it's written in the College Charter: if you're younger than sixteen when you die, you have to continue your education.'

'But why?' I asked in disgust. I thought I'd avoided it with Sir Syl and his 'Poetry'.

'Because you have to be prepared for this life, or should I say, this death!' She grinned at me. 'And study archery, fencing, spear-throwing, astronomy, history and...boar-hunting,' she said, almost choking as she laughed, and swallowed a strawberry, at the same time.

'History?' I said. 'It's bad enough having to learn about dead people, but being taught by dead people about dead people, now that's really weird.'

'It's good to do these things,' said Fi, matter-of-factly, 'just like we eat, even though we don't have to, and wear clothes to feel normal.'

'Normal?' I said. 'What's normal about people's noses, ears, even arms dropping off without notice?'

Right on cue, Dr. Dodo's left eyeball popped, unceremoniously, onto the table and rolled innocently towards me. It came to a gentle halt beside my fork.

'Look at that,' I whispered, 'did you ever see a more disgusting sight?'

Delicately licking the last of the cream from his hands, Dr. Josiah Funkelweede silently slipped his eyeball back into its socket. He flashed me an almost ghoulish ghostly smile and reached for the last slice of meringue.

'Get used to it, Simon,' said Fi, shrugging her shoulders. 'By the way, have you had other, more *pleasant* death experiences?'

'No,' I admitted slowly, 'this is my first time.'

'Then I rest my case,' she said, turning to talk to her mother.

All the feasting ghosts looked up as the Provost slapped *The Book of Ornis* on the table. A faint sigh escaped from its pages, as if it objected to this type of treatment. But it wasn't the sigh that caught my attention. It was the peculiar sight of Gauntley's detached hand lying on top of the Book. It wriggled slightly, as if it was happy to have suddenly gained independence from its owner. I saw Gauntley eyeing me. The seconds ticked by. Without warning, he grabbed the offending hand and pushed it back into place, with the familiar squelching noise his attaching nose had made. He then resumed talking to his wife and daughter, as if nothing had happened.

Fi didn't appear to notice. For her, it was like a dry twig dropping from a tree, but I wasn't convinced; I'd never get used to it.

To pass the time, I observed Mrs. Honeydew, sitting across from me, flanked by Brother Tobias and Pastor Longhorne. It was clear, as the evening progressed, she was becoming increasingly flustered. On her right, Brother Tobias enthusiastically preached the medicinal virtues of his home-brewed mead, and on her left, the Pastor preached the evils of drink. Unable to make a decision, she agreed with both, and took furtive sips on the rare occasion the Pastor looked the other way.

Miss Augusta Smithering-Smythe sat the other side of Dr. Dodo and I discovered that by pushing my chair back, I could talk to her. It was difficult to get used to her mad purple outfit and, several times, I thought her stuffed-cat hat winked at me. I wondered if I should wink back. I also got the distinct impression it had whiskers, but that may have been the poor lighting. 'Did I tell you, Simon,' she shouted above the steadily growing din, 'before I died, I studied Women's Education in the 1920s? A riveting subject and…'

'Augusta,' I interjected, before she was in full flow, 'why is the table moving…and…why is it so big?'

With an almost steady hand, she pushed her glasses onto her nose and, surprisingly, they stayed there for a full five minutes. 'Cadaver has always been known for its hospitality.

In 1753 there weren't enough places at a Feast. The Provost at the time, one Humpledork Stoner, had it inscribed in the College Charter that in future, we'd only use a round table and it would expand to fit whatever number turned up,' she smiled. 'But,' continued Augusta, 'in 1934, due to a clerical error, the entire town was invited to a Feast; five thousand of them. And they all came! Naturally, this threw the college into chaos; nobody knew what to do to avoid disaster! As you see, this table was designed to revolve, but with so large a crowd, some weren't fed for weeks, and a few of the unluckier guests starved to death as their plate only came around once. Fights broke out because the hungry townees simply decided to take any plate or didn't know which one was actually theirs. It was more a Famine than a Feast on that occasion and it certainly didn't help Town and Gown relations. Some from the town even claimed it was a college ruse to obtain cheap cadavers for research purposes. The Provost forbade large gatherings after that.'

But tonight, most of the ghosts were better behaved, and very well fed. The creatures from the Book were having some difficulties though: the woman with two heads choked several times, trying to feed both her mouths at once, and the executioner's headless victims spent several hours lifting food to their non-existent heads. They seemed very confused. The giants continually sneaked roast potatoes (and the odd whole turkey) into their cavernous handbags. At the dessert stage, entire lemon meringue pies, and several family-sized trifles, followed the turkeys. At least now I knew why they carried the handbags, though I still wasn't certain if the bag-toting giants were male or female.

All things considered, on this occasion, there didn't seem to be the remotest chance of anyone breaking into open warfare. And I was getting used to the system; if your plate only appeared every ten minutes or so, then the Feast became a much more relaxed affair and there was plenty of time to chat between bites.

To Augusta's left, the Porter blew his nose noisily at regular intervals, occasionally interjecting with comments such as 'no-good laggard' directed at me, and 'the kitchen is the only place for a woman...' at Augusta.

Finally, the Assistant Librarian could bear it no longer and gave the Porter a very long (and very stiff) lecture on suffragettes and the suffragette movement. 'I was famishing, chained to the railings. So cold, in fact, I got pneumonia and died. At least,' she sniffed, 'I died for a cause.' This was a direct hit at the Porter as it was well know he'd fallen asleep in the gutter, after a day at the races, and had never woken again.

'Sire,' whispered a voice behind me.

I turned to see Sir Syl fumbling beneath his armour, a look of intense concentration on his face and muttering something about 'Taking this heaven-sent opportunity to read my new creation.'

I suppressed a groan. It had been great to get away from him for a day or two.

'It's called, "I Adore Thy Smallpoxed Face",' he announced and with a flourish triumphantly fished out a crumpled sheet of parchment from deep inside his armour.

'My noble charger, Tiberius, did chew on it, Sire, as I contemplated its unrivalled magnificence.'

I believed him, as the parchment definitely showed signs of ill treatment; large teeth marks and grass stains. Yet I seriously doubted it would be magnificent.

'It's for Odette,' continued the knight, 'a parlour-maid who died three hundred years ago of the smallpox. But who is no less beautiful to me, Sire, because of so slight an impediment.' A ghost with only half a face, sitting at the other end of the table, blushed furiously.

'Later, Sir Syl,' I begged.

He was crestfallen but moved away without another word, still clutching his poem.

The noise level rose as the assembled ghosts continued to tuck into the gastronomic delights. From the appreciative slurping, grunting and burping, it wasn't difficult to work out that the ghosts were enjoying themselves enormously. Flagons of Brother Tobias's Best Mead were eagerly passed round, and the more the ghosts consumed, the louder the party became.

I located Gusty by the clouds of black smoke that billowed, chimney-like, from the other side of the table. I was fascinated to see smoke pouring from his navel area and his ears. Brundelwicke sat beside him. He was so tiny his eyes were level with the table and as a result missed his plate several times, as it came round. However, a few minutes later, he'd fallen asleep, and gently snored, his forehead bumping on the table, as it continued to rotate.

The Jester was nowhere to be seen, but then, he had no teeth to eat with!

And I was surprised to see Ernest Coddle, but I suppose even a habitual scribbler had to eat sometime. A stack of yellowed pages tottered dangerously beside his plate and as they passed he'd grab his quill and write frantically.

'Ernest!' rapped out the Provost from across the table. Ernest's head suddenly jerked up. His unkempt hair straggled around his pale face and rested, greatly resembling a bird's nest, on his shoulders. There were dark rings under his eyes.

'You can't write at the Feast!'

'I have no time,' said Ernest in a frantic voice. 'No time…'

I had to find out what he was writing.

Then I overheard the Pirate Queen protesting to Gauntley, 'But, Rufus, my powers have waned, I have only barely managed to bring our Fiain back. You know I must return to Atlantis tonight. My people need me.'

The Pirate Queen then turned to Fi. 'Hildebrande…you know the power it contains…the wielder can only kill an enemy, never a friend. If you try to kill a friend, it will turn and kill you. Always remember to use it wisely, my child.'

I leaned closer to hear more. Hildebrande and the Gael Magic fascinated me, and I was sorry that Fi's mother would soon be leaving.

Gauntley rose slowly to his feet and tapped his glass with a spoon. 'And now we'll sing the college anthem.'

The ghosts all stood to attention and began to sing:

Hoorah, hoorah, Cadaver wears the Crown
Hoorah, hoorah, we love to wear the Gown
In our annual battle, with the stinking Town
We are the best and always beat them down!

Everyone cheered. But I had no idea what the anthem was about, and I didn't get a chance to ask, because the Porter bent over clutching his stomach and screamed, 'It's me innards! It's me innards, innit?'

Then all hell broke loose.

Chapter 21

The Attack

Just as Fi was saying, 'Ignore him, he doesn't have any innards,' a loud explosion erupted in the darkness overhead. It was followed by petrified screams and, suddenly, we were thrown to the ground, at least twenty feet from where we'd been sitting. The table, and everything on it, flew into the air, then landed, smashing into smithereens, adding to the ghosts' injuries and general mayhem. Out of the corner of my eye, I could see Gauntley lying motionless where he'd fallen. And he wasn't the only one. Fi and I both scrambled, shocked and shaken, to our feet.

Beside us, blue lightning bolts flew in every direction from the outstretched hands of the Pirate Queen, her long, grey-streaked hair flying as she darted left and right, trying to get a good angle to kill our attackers. The impressive lightning bolts must be the powerful Gael Magic I'd longed to see, my numbed brain told me, as I tried to push my way through the screaming, panicking crowd to Gauntley. There were ghosts shoving in every direction, passing through each other (a creepy and painful experience for a ghost), and falling over those lying on the ground. A barrage of explosions filled the air and, as far as I could tell, on the ground as well. There was a horrible smell of burning. We were under attack!

'Giant bats,' shouted someone.

Then, a familiar baying noise shattered the night air. It would've made my blood run cold if I had any – Halbizia's hell-hounds. But that wasn't all. Hundreds of vast-winged missiles began to dive-bomb us in a vicious and sustained attack. There was another huge explosion, directly overhead, and I was again thrown to the ground. I hit my head and when I tried to sit up, the world was spinning and there was a crushing weight on top of me.

'Sire…'

'Sir Syl?' I gasped, barely able to breathe. 'Is that you?'

'My steed, Sire…my humblest apologies…'

'Get him off!' I managed to say, and then remembered he only had one arm!

I heard a great deal of puffing and shouting of instructions, and finally Sir Syl's horse was removed to reveal Brother Tobias panting, his barrel-chest rising and falling rapidly, and several of the undergraduates, also out of breath. Sir Syl looked distraught. His favourite charger lay dead at his feet. It was unlucky for me that the ghosts of animals weighed heavier than those of humans.

'If only I hadn't brought Tiberius with me to the college…' he moaned.

But I hadn't time to listen; wave after wave of vicious creatures still attacked us from the air. Finally, one dropped at my feet, as dead as one of Funkelweede's dodos, an electric green charge scorching its fur, giving off a horrible singed smell. It was a turkey-sized bat, its enormous wingspan stretched out in death, giving it a vulture-like appearance. I had no idea they made so much noise, their collective squeaks and screeching continuing to fill the chilly night air. There were thousands of them. Had Halbizia got reinforcements? I shuddered as I tried to catch my breath.

Then two enormous, charcoal-grey hell-hounds, their yellow fangs bared, charged into the main body of the screaming crowd, many of which were rooted to the spot, frozen with terror. Their deadly fangs bit legs, arms and throats, ripping the terrified ghosts to pieces. Screams and shrieks joined the noise of the bats and the overhead bombs continued unabated. One of the hell-hounds, as big as a pony, reared on his enormous hind legs and growled into my face, his heavy front paws pinning me to the library wall. His frenzied red-coloured eyes bored into mine and I knew, without doubt, this was the end. For some reason I kept my eyes open. I've never known why, but it saved my ghostly life.

Instead of ripping my throat out as I fully expected, the hound's eyes grew sleepy. It blinked once or twice, rolled off me and loped away, as docile as a lapdog. I just stared after it, paralysed with fear, barely able to believe I'd escaped.

Sir Syl gaped in astonishment, 'Sire, thou art an animal-trainer, a stupefier of animals, a...' but just then, a particularly enormous giant bat swooped down on us, narrowly missing me. It caught Sir Syl in its cruel talons, and bore him away, before I could even cry out. In a few short seconds, the bat and Sir Syl were tiny black dots in the chilly night sky. And then, even with the light of the full moon, I could no longer see the Crusader at all.

Sir Syl was gone, and his beloved charger was dead! I sat down heavily on the cobbles. I couldn't believe it. Yes, he was a pest and every day I wished he was somewhere else – anywhere else – just to give me a few minutes' peace. Yet I never really wanted him kidnapped, as Halbizia's prisoner…or worse.

Glancing round, I saw that the attack was easing off. The terrible noise had given way to infrequent screeches. The Pirate Queen, blue bolts still flying from her outstretched hands, was seeing off the last of the bats, and the hell-hounds had disappeared. Fi stood beside her mother, having fought through the mêlée to her side. I could see that they were badly shaken, and many of the Cadaver ghosts were in a sorry state.

A high-pitched woman's scream rang out. I knew instantly it was Mrs. Honeydew. Still feeling the after-effects of Tiberius's great weight, I floated as fast as I could in the matron's direction, with Fi and the Pirate Queen close on my heels. We found Mrs. Honeydew kneeling over Gauntley's body; *it was glaringly obvious he was dead.* And now I understood the full implications of dying as a ghost.

Fi staggered and her mother caught her. She began to cry in great gasping sobs, her father's body at her feet. I stared in disbelief. Surely this couldn't have happened? It felt like a terrible nightmare. Then I found myself by Fi's side, though I didn't recollect having moved there.

'He's dead!' cried the Pirate Princess. 'He's dead!' There was no doubt about it, looking at his arms spread-eagled and his wide-open unseeing eyes. The Pirate Queen comforted Fi, while staring in total disbelief at her dead husband.

The ghosts who'd fled indoors during the onslaught slowly began to make their way out and form a circle around the dead Provost. Many wept when they saw Gauntley. However, he wasn't the only one; three young students had also died in the brutal and unprovoked attack. Soon all the bodies ceased to be and faded to nothing. Fi wept in her mother's arms and I couldn't help thinking she'd got her mother back only to lose her father and I knew, without asking, she was devastated. All the ghosts looked stunned and shocked. A few looked angry.

And Mrs. Honeydew, Dr. Dodo and at least a dozen others were injured. I could already see they were missing limbs, or had large rents and tears in their bodies, and their ashen faces told their own story. Would they survive or cease to be? It was anybody's guess.

As we carried the wounded to Darwin's laboratory, I couldn't help noticing the broken Feast table, the charred bodies of dead bats, the torn academic gowns and what looked suspiciously like Miss Smithering-Smythe's trampled hat on the cobblestones. Only an hour ago we were enjoying the party. I wished I could escape from the sea-witch, but it never seemed to work out like that.

Chapter 22

The Funeral

The days and nights that followed were terrible. The entire college was in mourning for Gauntley, not only the man, but our leader and head of the college. I could tell from the worried faces of the college ghosts that they felt the same way, but they also mourned for the dead undergraduates. It was a lot to lose in one attack. *And* there was no sign of Sir Syl. I had no time to think, nor did I actually want to, of my own narrow escape from the hell-hound, or how it had come about.

Fi was now paler than ever. The Pirate Queen had made it known she was planning to leave after the funerals, as she'd expended all her remaining energy during the fight. It was now so dangerously depleted she had to return to Atlantis immediately, or risk dying as a ghost herself. Indeed, she looked so faded and weak, I thought she'd disappear before our eyes. A further messenger had arrived to hasten her departure.

Then there were the practicalities of the funerals. I didn't know what to expect, never having attended a ghostly one, but it wasn't at all what I imagined. The day after the attack, the entire college and the creatures from *The Book of Ornis,* assembled at noon at the Campanile. The college bells tolled for what seemed like an age. Perhaps it was my imagination, but it felt mistier and colder than any other day since my arrival. All the college ghosts were sombre and wore their darkest clothes. There had been genuine affection for the Provost.

Many of them spoke for a few moments about the deceased, and without exception, they praised the Provost and the three undergraduates. But it was Fi's words that haunted me most.

I barely recognized her in a dress, standing beside her remaining parent. 'He was great,' she said, her voice quivering, but with her head held high, '...just great.' Then she gulped, once or twice, and her mother gave her a hug. The Pirate Queen spoke more eloquently but with no less feeling. 'He was a singular man who achieved much in life and death. He will be greatly missed.' A respectful silence followed.

Finally, a white feather for each of the dead was passed through the crowd. 'It symbolizes that their life as a ghost is now over,' Mrs. Honeydew whispered to me, her eyes swollen and red. She'd cried quietly into her lace handkerchief throughout the entire funeral. Her left arm hung in a sling.

Then very slowly, and with great dignity, the entire procession moved to the Provosts' Graveyard for the final part of the funeral for Professor Gantley. Not for a burial, of course, as there were no bodies to bury; but for a new inscription on his headstone, noting his second and final death. As the Porter scratched the date with a quill, I was surprised to see there was genuine sadness etched on his features.

'He'd have been proud of that,' said Fi, her eyes bright, floating up beside me. 'He loved the college and the Provost's Graveyard is elevated. I'm sure he'll be happy with the view.' It was a good view of the college, but I didn't like to mention I felt doubtful that her father could see it.

Again, very slowly, the procession continued to the Student's Graveyard and we waited as the Porter inscribed the three headstones. It had been agreed to leave Sir Syl's for the moment, as he was only missing and not dead – at least as far as we knew.

All in all, it was a sad funeral. Almost the saddest I had ever attended. But the partings weren't over yet.

'I only came to Cadaver to recover you,' I overheard the Pirate Queen say gently to her daughter, a tear sliding down her cheek. I hadn't realized a Pirate Queen, especially one of Gráinne's fearsome reputation, could cry. 'Your father was a good man,' she said sadly. 'Halbizia has much to answer for.'

'Atlantis needs you, Your Highness…Mother,' said Fi. 'Don't feel bad about leaving.'

'This is something *you* have to do, on your own. Never forget you are a Pirate Princess and someday you will be Queen. Remember all I've taught you.' Fi nodded sadly, her eyes never leaving her mother's face. 'You have Hildebrande… and you know its powers.'

'You should take it back,' said Fi, in a small voice, 'it's yours…'

'But you have the greatest need, my dear daughter. Hildebrande is a precious gift that has come down through our forebears, and there is no other I would entrust it to. May it protect you from all harm. I have my pirates and the Gael Magic.'

There was a flash of blue and she disappeared.

The suddenness of her departure took us all by surprise. I could see Fi struggling not to cry and it was impossible not to feel sorry for her. It must be hard to be reunited with your mother and then lose her in the space of a couple of days, and then lose your father for good. I suddenly missed Sir Syl and it struck me that he might never return. I might never hear his awful poetry again.

'Is that the ghost of a smile, Simon?' asked Brother Tobias who was passing.

'I was just thinking of "I Adore Thy Smallpoxed Face", Sir Syl's last poem. I was wondering what it would have been like. He never got a chance to read it at the Feast.'

Brother Tobias stopped to consider this. 'Terrible, I should think,' he said, 'just like all the others.'

I had to agree but the thought cheered me up a little. Perhaps he wasn't dead. He would simply bore Halbizia to death with his poetry and then escape. Perhaps he'd soon be boring us again. I glanced at the large bottle of *BEST MEAD* tucked under the Monk's arm.

'It's medicinal,' he said hurriedly, 'for the patients. I'm on my way to see them. This stuff will put hair on their chests.'

I was a bit startled to hear this. 'I suppose if that's what they want…' I said, thinking that perhaps the females might not be happy with this development.

'Yes,' mused the not-overly-concerned Brother, 'though sometimes people do seem to have an adverse reaction to it.'

The Porter clutching his stomach at the Feast immediately sprang to mind. 'The Porter…?'

'Yes,' he said with a heavy sigh, 'I fear what he drank didn't agree with him. I tried to warn him but there's no reasoning with a man like that.'

It made me laugh again just to think of the Porter clutching his 'innards'. At least there was still something to laugh at.

****

But after a night filled with bizarre dreams of Sir Syl flying through the air on Tiberius, then disappearing into blue clouds, and Gauntley telling me I had to practise conversing with hell-hounds, I awoke early the next morning feeling awful. Yet I couldn't lie in bed and decided to see if there were other early risers, though it would have been understandable if the college ghosts had decided to have a quiet day in their rooms. To my surprise, I heard Fi before I saw her. She was practising duelling, as normal, and Sir Syl's statue, which had strangely recovered from previous assaults, was getting its usual battering. Her normal baggy clothes had replaced yesterday's dress. She seemed a little more herself, though I noticed she gripped Hildebrande tighter than usual.

'Hi,' I said when she finally turned to look at me. I suspected she knew I was there all along, but it was difficult for her to face me after yesterday. I felt the same. 'Death does that,' my mother had said before my father's funeral, 'it makes conversation difficult.' But then I thought: *Fi and I are old hands at this: we've done this before; we're both dead.*

Fortunately, I had an idea. 'I'm going to see the wounded. D'you want to come?'

To my surprise, she nodded, sheathed Hildebrande (to my relief) and we floated to the library. I thought it might cheer her up to see Darwin again. And it did slightly, even if it was upsetting to see so many wounded, despite his best efforts to patch them up. He whispered to me that he thought most would survive. Seven creatures from the Book had been injured, though many weren't in good shape to begin with. It occurred to me they had no hope of becoming their real selves now Gráinne had returned to Atlantis. What would become of them? I judged by the looks on their faces, that they were thinking the same thing themselves.

As we left, Fi turned to me, and held up Hildebrande. 'On this cutlass I'll avenge my father's death. I'll kill the sea-witch if it's the last thing I do.'

And from the look on her face I believed her.

TO BE CONTINUED...

With Gauntley dead, is Simon up to the challenge of leading Cadaver College, in a fight to-the-death, against the evil sea-witch Halbizia? Find out in:

The Curse of Halbizia

Dare to read on...

Chapter 1

My Speech to the College

Two days after the Provost's funeral, Dr. Funkelweede, as the oldest remaining Council member, called an emergency meeting of the College Council, to be held in Front Square. He'd asked me particularly to attend. I was curious as to why he'd singled me out, though I'd heard that most of college would be there. This development really brought home to me the gravity of our situation, that the college was still under Halbizia's curse, and particularly that we no longer had the Provost's wisdom and experience to guide us. Who'd be the new Provost? And, most importantly, would he or she, lead us in the fight against Halbizia?

The meeting kicked off at midday beneath a sparkling blue sky. Surrounded by the now familiar college buildings and the neatly cut lawns of the squares, it was almost impossible to believe the chaos and terror of the recent attack in the same spot. Only the odd scorch marks on some of the statues indicated anything had happened. However, the assembled ghosts' troubled faces told a different story as we waited, in a semicircle, facing the library. Dr. Dodo, as the college's oldest academic, stood on the steps, a bent old man in a black gown which flapped in the gentle breeze. As he raised his arms he reminded me of an old, black crow. And he didn't sound much better; he wittered on about the college, its glorious history and how it would be more even glorious in the future. I sensed he was moving rapidly onto his favourite subject when a student shouted:

'We need a speech with aplomb.'

The Porter, as moth-eaten as usual and clutching his ever-present lamp, stood between me and the student. He immediately snarled, 'Who are yer callin' a plum, yer young whipper-snapper? I was niver a plum in ma life.'

'He was talking to Dr. Funkelweede...' I explained, trying not to laugh. 'Aplomb...not a plum.'

'Plums niver agreed with ma innards...' he began, but was immediately interrupted by shouts from the crowd.

'Simon, Simon...' they called, 'we want Simon...'

I couldn't believe my ears. *Why were they calling me?*

'Speech, speech...'

Somebody pushed me forward, and as I floated towards the steps, I noticed the Porter wore an indecipherable expression; but there was nothing new about that. All the other ghosts smiled and nodded encouragement.

'You can do it, Simon,' whispered Darwin in my ear as I passed. I nodded as if agreeing with him; however, my legs

151

were numb and if my heart could still beat, it would be hammering in my chest right now.

I made it to the platform, yet looking out at the vast sea of faces a surge of panic threatened to overwhelm me. What was I doing up here and what did they want me to say or do for that matter? Yet even as I asked myself these questions, I knew the answers. I knew because it was all I'd thought of since I'd released the Pirate Queen and, in doing so, saved Fi. And since Gauntley's death, it seemed almost ordained that I take his place. I was a de Bruin after all and I was here to fight Halbizia. If I had to become Provost to achieve that end, so be it. And, if my efforts ended in my own ghostly death, then at least I'd have given it my best shot; I wouldn't have let the de Bruins down…

Check-out my blog on
www.chroniclesofcadavercollege.com

Acknowledgements

Margaret, thank you for your help and encouragement. I couldn't have done it without you.

Vikki, you are fantastic. Your bubbly enthusiasm is infectious!

My friends, what can I say? You're the best and thanks for always being there: Hilary, Alison, Daphne, Heather, Mary O'Sullivan, Jean, Mary Ward, Sandra, Kathleen, Charis, Elva, Brigid, Jessica, May, Brenda and Roisin.

Charis, Daphne and Gareth, you are brilliant editors, the mistakes are all mine...

Tony, Steve and Ion, you delivered on your promises, thank you.

Emma, Caroline and Jonathan, my nieces and nephews...you're great!

Tom and Walter, my brothers-in-law...you take some beating!

My readers, Jack, Dylan (and all the others)...you were fabulous.

The children of Crookstown Primary School, it has been a lot of fun reading to you. Thank you to Jacqui, and all the teachers, for having me.

I really enjoyed meeting, and reading to, everyone in Ballinlough Primary School, Co. Meath and the Cosby National School, Stradbally, Co. Laois.

Finally, thanks to Seán Malone, for a beautifully designed cover.